To Marsha R. Puz

From,
    Mom and Dad

On my 10th birthday
    Dec. 1, 1962

Horses, *Horses*, HORSES

Horses,

Horses, HORSES

PALOMINOS AND
PINTOS,
POLO PONIES AND
PLOW HORSES,
MORGANS AND
MUSTANGS

Selected by PHYLLIS R. FENNER
Illustrated by PERS CROWELL

Franklin Watts, *Inc.*
575 Lexington Avenue, New York 22, N. Y.

Designed by BERT CLARKE

Manufactured in the United States of America

Acknowledgments

To Paul Annixter and Story Parade, Inc. for *Champion of the Peaks,* by Paul Annixter from Story Parade Magazine. Copyright 1948 by the author.

To Random House, Inc. for *The Match Race,* from *Black Stallion,* by Walter Farley. Copyright 1941. Reprinted by special permission of the publisher.

To Story Parade, Inc. for the following stories reprinted by permission from Story Parade Magazine: *King of the Range,* by Margaret Jamison, copyright 1947; *The Royal Greens,* by Russell Gordon Carter, copyright 1940; *Can a Horse Know Too Much?* by Genevieve Torrey Eames, copyright 1945; *Such a Kind World,* by Mabel Leigh Hunt, copyright 1946.

To Charles Scribner's Sons for the following stories, used by permission of the publishers: *The Squeak of Leather* from *Smoky,* by Will James, copyright 1926; *The Pacing Mustang* from *Wild Animals I Have Known,* by Ernest Thompson Seton. Copyright, 1896 by Charles Scribner's Sons; 1926 by Ernest Thompson Seton.

To Alfred A. Knopf, Inc. for *Scott Makes Good,* reprinted from *Frog,* by Col. S. P. Meek, by permission of Alfred A. Knopf, Inc. Copyright 1933 by Alfred A. Knopf, Inc.

To Gladys Lewis and Copp Clark, Ltd., Toronto, for *The Black Stallion and the Red Mare* from Story Parade Magazine. Copyright 1945 by the publisher.

To Macmillan Company, Inc. for *High Courage* from *High Courage* by C. W. Anderson. Copyright 1941 by The Macmillan Company; *Mohawk Makes a Comeback* from *Salute,* by C. W. Anderson. Copyright 1940 by The Macmillan Company, Inc.

To Oxford University Press for *Bucephalus* from *Each in His Way,* by Alice Gall and Fleming Crew. Copyright 1937 by Oxford University Press. Used by permission of the publishers.

To Harcourt, Brace and Company for *The Cutter Race* reprinted from *Red Horse Hill*, by Stephen W. Meader. Copyright 1930 by Harcourt, Brace and Company. Used by permission of the publishers.

To Longmans, Green and Company for the following stories: *Death Dive* from *Prairie Colt*, by Stephen Holt. Copyright 1947 by Longmans, Green and Company; *Roping Contest* from *Wild Palomino*, by Stephen Holt. Copyright 1946 by Longmans, Green and Company.

To Julian Messner, Inc. for *Jarvis Discovers Gold*, reprinted by permission of Julian Messner, Inc. from *A Horse to Remember* by Genevieve Torrey Eames. Copyright 1947 by Genevieve Torrey Eames.

To David McKay Company, Inc. for *Corral Walls* from *Beyond Rope and Fence*, by David Grew. Copyright 1947 by David McKay Company.

Contents

Illustrations

Daffy over HORSES

"Wouldn't go to an auto show.
She preferred a rodeo . . .
  because she's
Crazy over
  horses, horses, horses.
Nutty over
  horses, horses, horses, horses . . ." *

THAT GIRL who is "goofy over horses" isn't alone in her love. There are fifty million others just as goofy, and you are one of them. It's a nice love, whatever kind of horse. The little orphan children loved the plough horse just as intensely as Bud loved Cedar, or Peter loved the lame race horse, Mohawk, or Jarvis loved the homely little colt that turned out to be pure gold. The love of horses is a very ancient one. Even the gods had their winged breed. Folk tales are full of horses, their wisdom and loyalty. The story of Alexander and Bucephalus, which you will read here, is as old as history almost.

Here are a few good stories about different kinds of horses. Some of them you will recognize. Others you will meet for the first time. All of them you will love.

P. F.

* From the popular song HORSES by Byron Gay and Richard A. Whiting. Copyright 1926 by Leo Feist, Inc. Used by Special Permission of Copyright Proprietor.

Horses, *Horses*, HORSES

∘ 1 ∘

CHAMPIONS OF THE PEAKS

by PAUL ANNIXTER

SLIPPY HIMSELF was primarily to blame for what happened that fall day. He had always been a bit too independent for his own good, and since his friendship with old Sounder, the ranch dog, had sprung up, he'd been a constant worry to Jesse Hunnicutt.

Slipstream, he was called—Slippy for short—and he'd been named for his speed. His hide was the color of running bronze. When in action, with flying mane and wild of eye and nostril, his head might have been that of Pegasus the winged. He was only a two-year-old, but already the pride of High Ranch. Some day, Jesse Hunnicutt believed, Slippy would be as good as any of the champion polo ponies he had raised.

There was nothing really bad about Slippy. He was just too full of ideas and pranks which walled him off from serious training. Sometimes in his wide-browed skull a cunning brain seemed bent on mischief—at least, so Jake Marden, the ranch foreman, claimed. Let a day dawn when a visiting buyer was to appear and Slippy

17

would disappear up the mountain. As High Ranch was fenceless open range there was little to be done about this, unless someone remembered to lock Slippy in the barn.

It was old Sounder who had really gotten Slippy into the habit of these disappearances. He was the special property of young Jesse, who was fifteen, and old Jesse's only son. Part Walker, with an admixture of mastiff in his blood, Sounder had a seamed and melancholy face, big bones, great lubberly paws, and the heart of a lion. No respecter of bounds or barriers was Sounder, but a privileged character who spent a great share of his days on the heights, tracking rabbit, fox, or wild cat.

Slippy had met Sounder one day in spring far up among the pinon pines. They had smelled noses and each had belonged specially to the other from there on in. They had met often after that, up there in the peaks, far from the sounds and scents of the ranch. Sometimes the pair would remain away for two days and two nights running, dependent upon one another for company and moral support; Slippy feeding and rolling in some cup between the peaks where the grass grew lush all summer, Sounder digging for marmots on a near-by slope or tracking rabbits in the brush, till darkness brought them close together. Great days for them both.

Alone, Slippy would never have had the initiative for such forays, but with Sounder to lead the way, the long wanderings among the crags were an endless adventure. At such times, with all the animals' wild instincts uppermost, not even young Jesse or old Jesse himself could get near the two when they happened to sight them among the peaks.

18

So it was on the November day in question. For some time knife-edged blasts of wind had warned of bad weather close at hand, but Jesse Hunnicutt had elected to stay at High Ranch till snow actually fell. Then one morning the ranch hands awoke at dawn with a norther sobbing through the cracks and chinks of the bunkhouse and a sting of sleet in the air. Dun clouds hung low over the peaks and the valleys were lost in a smudgy haze. There was not an hour to spare if they expected to get stock and equipment to the lowlands in time to escape the oncoming blizzard.

Slippy and Sounder were missing again. Both had been away overnight, and old Jesse muttered profanely as he scanned the high trails. Within an hour gear and stock were ready to move, and still no sign of the runaways. Grudgingly Jesse gave the order to leave, but he himself rode up-trail a way for one last look for Slipstream. Young Jesse followed on Uncle, a solid, sure-footed piebald.

For nearly an hour the two searched and called into the teeth of the wind, but to no avail. Slippy and Sounder were far up the mountain at the time, taking refuge in the lee of a rock ledge. Old Jesse hated to abandon the search, not the least of his reasons being the loss of one of the most promising horses ever raised on High Ranch. For when he turned his mount down-trail that day he never expected to see Slipstream alive again, though he hid the fact from his son.

"We'll come back when the weather breaks and look for them again, son,' he placated. "Old Sounder'll come through, never fear. But we've got to go now, or we'll never get down the mountain."

19

When the storm broke shortly before dawn, Slip-stream was sheltered in a high spruce grove where he had spent a chilly and restless night. Sounder was afar, engaged in his endless game of digging out mountain marmots, and now and then coursing after snowshoe rabbits. Slippy could hear him from time to time, sounding his hoarse bell-like hunting cry.

By the time the sleet had turned to driving snow, Sounder gave up his splendid game and sought his friend among the trees. When morning came with the storm increasing, uneasiness began to ride the pair. What feeding there was had already been covered with snow. Slippy's thoughts turned to the warmth and security of the great barns at High Ranch. He had had enough for a time of this fodderless freedom. So, too, had Sounder. But when their steps turned down-trail and they emerged from the shelter of the spruce, they were almost swept from their feet by the sheer force of the gale. In places the snow was already belly-deep on Sounder, and everything familiar about the landscape had been obliterated.

Sounder and Slipstream pressed on, heads bent to the blast. Trails were gone. Only their sure feet and their wild instincts kept them to the right way. On the steep slopes they slipped and scrambled precariously, then picked a slow and dextrous course along a mile of shelving rock ledges that pinched off into space. Later it was an even greater battle bucking through the drifts of the sheltered places.

It was far past midday when they sighted the ranch buildings and Slippy experienced one of his first great shocks. The ranch was deserted. Not a trace of smoke rose from the ranch-house chimneys, and there were not even any fresh tracks to show which way the men had gone.

Behind the summer lean-to the two took refuge and there Slippy found a few wisps of hay and straw in the long feed trough. Still others he uncovered by pawing the snowy ground beneath. Somewhat heartened by these mementos of man he settled down, eyes half closed, sensitive ears a-twitch, to await the ranchers' return. But Sounder had no such illusions. He prowled forlornly, whining with a growing unrest.

All that day the storm continued. Slippy finished every last sprig of hay in the lean-to. As the darkness of another night, hostile and smothering, descended on the mountain wilderness, he lifted his voice in sharp, imperative neighs. But no one came.

Through the dark hours the two runaways huddled together for warmth. When another day dawned with no lessening of the storm, loneliness and growing fear gripped Slippy. All that day the two waited and shivered in a world filled with storm, cold, and misery. But no one came, and through a second stormy night they pressed together for very life's sake, their coats covered with a thickening layer of frost and snow.

By noon of the third day the storm had subsided. Sounder set off down the mountain, whither he knew the ranch hands had gone. Slippy fell in behind him. The snow by now had piled belly-high on the horse and in two hours the pair progressed scarcely a mile, with the going harder every yard. Twice Slippy almost pitched into oblivion over the sheer cliffs; at last he turned back up the trail. Sounder followed him, for each was bound to the other now by ties as deep as life.

When hunger drove them forth from the lean-to again, it was up the mountain instead of down, for on the heights the snow was far less deep. In places the ridges were swept almost bare by the force of the wind. Up along the sparse spruce valleys they plodded, Slippy finding here and there some uncovered forage, and chewing many evergreen twigs for good measure. Sounder ran rabbits through the thickets.

Later that afternoon Slippy came upon a small herd of deer banded together in a winter "yard." Moved by an urge for companionship, he moved forward eagerly to join them, but the two leading bucks of the herd shook menacing heads.

Slippy was too forlorn and miserable to care what the deer thought of him. Even ill feeling was preferable to the empty loneliness of the peaks. He waited meekly, some fifty paces away, to see what would happen.

The snow roundabout was too deep for the deer to flee their yard, so the bucks contented themselves with stampings and repeated challenges. But Slippy had a disarming way of his own. He ruckled softly in his chest, and after an hour or so his quiet presence broke down resistance. The deer resumed their sketchy feeding, nibbling at the hanging branches of the trees and pawing down to the sparse feeding beneath the snow.

Later, when Sounder came in from a successful hunt, the deer were thrown into fresh panic. In fall or summer the deer would have fled like shadows and Sounder would have given chase in wild abandon. Now he came up meek and silent as Slippy himself and dropped panting beside his friend. Before long even his presence was accepted by the deer, for a magic truce had descended upon all.

By the time darkness came, horse and dog were learning the shelter and warmth that lies in snow when one is wise enough to burrow into it.

Each of the next four days they visited the ranch house, returning to the heights in the afternoon. Then on the fourth day they returned to find their wild friends had moved. The feeding had given out in the vicinity of the yard, and the deer had left to seek a better sanctuary.

Slippy followed along their trail, laboring slowly through the deep snow. He came upon the herd again a half mile away, tramping out a new yard which was to become a tragic prison for all of them. A thaw the next day was followed by another snowstorm. The high walls of the deer yard froze to the hardness of concrete, forming a prison from which there was no escape until another thaw.

Only Slippy's restlessness and his persistent urge to find his human friends saved him from sharing the fate of the deer. He was keeping vigil again at the ranch house when the freeze came. When he labored back to the deer yard he was unable to join his friends as usual. An iron crust had formed over the snow, and the pony stood nearly seven feet above the yard, looking dejectedly down on his imprisoned friends.

After four days, the feeding in the yard was consumed and the deer grew leaner and leaner, until the does and younglings were so weak they could hardly stand. Still no thaw came to liberate them.

23

The slow drama ended in tragedy one night when a mountain lion discovered the starving herd.

What followed was swifter and more merciful than starvation. Death came to them all, in their prison of ice.

Slippy, growing woodswise and wary, was warned of the menace that threatened on the lean dawn wind. A faint rank smell had come creeping into his consciousness, the musty reek of mountain lion. He knew it though he had never scented it before, and even to his peaceful intelligence that taint meant death. It sent him scrambling wildly out of the woods and onto a cleared slope just above.

Two days later Slippy and Sounder returned to find what was left of their friends, the deer. At the sight of the frozen and half-devoured carcasses, they did not wait for any chance encounter with the cougar. Keeping close together, they left that part of the mountain far behind and climbed toward the frozen peaks of the Divide. Now, because of the cougar, they avoided the dense timber for the rest of that day and therefore went hungry. And to add to their misery, another snowstorm started toward nightfall.

It was morning of the third day, with Sounder hunting far below, when Slippy rounded an outcrop of rock high above timber line and had the surprise of his life. A dozen or more fleecy hummocks of snow suddenly came to life about a hundred feet ahead of him.

Slippy was staring at his first band of mountain goats. One of them, the biggest, with pale fierce eyes, had a long, frosted white beard and black horns curling above his head. He snoofed explosively in challenge while the others melted away behind him.

The goats, fifteen of them, fled up over the rims as Slippy moved forward, but they could not go far because of the drifted snow. Slippy pressed on, disregarding the loud snoofing challenges of the old leader, who sought to engage Slippy in combat. But it takes two to make any sort of battle. Finding nothing to vent his wrath upon, the old Billy subsided at last into an occasional angry snorting and stamping.

When Sounder approached in search of his friend, the whole goat band disappeared like magic beyond a seemingly unscalable peak, and Slippy thought he had lost them for good. But next morning he found them again.

When the band moved, Slippy followed silently in their wake, edging closer by degrees. When they uncovered the short cured grass of the heights and ate, he also ate and found it good. The goats began to look upon him as a friendly, harmless creature. By the third day Slippy was suffered to feed and bed at will on the edge of the band during the daytime hours when Sounder was hunting afar. But the dog they would not accept.

At night old Sounder always found Slippy, and the two slept together in some cranny out of the wind. But by day Slippy continued to follow the goats. He found their feeding lean fare, but it kept life in his body.

In the second week the goat leader led the band along a series of narrow, precipitous ledges to the distant peaks. Slippy's small, trim hoofs were becoming almost as sure as those of the goats themselves. Acrobatic feats, however, were a bit beyond him. The narrow ledge the band had been following pinched sharply off into space. But ten feet below it a two-foot nubbin of rock protruded from the face of the cliff. The old goat leaped for it, balanced a moment, then dropped to another still farther on, and thence to another narrow ledge beyond. One by one the rest of the goats followed suit.

Slippy stood at the end of the ledge looking miserably after them. He could not follow, or even turn around. Misery seized upon him and he lifted his voice in a protesting neigh. The goats, however, paid no heed. Already they were out of sight.

There was but one thing to do. Cautiously, feeling for each foothold, Slippy began backing along the ledge down which he had come. There were four hundred yards of that before he reached a spot where he could turn. Up over the rims he went by a roundabout way, but the goats were nowhere in sight.

For ten days thereafter Slippy wandered the heights, miserably searching for his friends along all the streets and avenues of the high goat cities. And each day two bald eagles sailed close to him expectantly, waiting for some mischance to strike him down. But Slippy, with a surprising ruggedness and craft, was doing the unbelievable—meeting and beating the winter wild in its cruelest and grimmest aspect.

A fighting spirit had awakened in him, a spirit that harked back to his hardy ancestors. His clever brain, that had formerly contrived small tricks of mischief, now worked overtime for self-protection. He had profited by all the object lessons of the deer and goats, and added numerous observations of his own. The fierce winds of the heights, he knew, could be depended upon to uncover enough herbage to keep life in his body, and at night he kept from freezing to death by huddling close to Sounder on the sheltered side of the peaks. But his civilized nature was dying the seven deaths in those mountain solitudes, and many times a day his lonesome whinny echoed among the crags.

Sounder too was doing the incredible, surpassing through necessity all normal bounds of his nature. Wolfish instincts came uppermost in him, instructing him how to consume enough snow for the water he needed, how to tell from afar when a deep snowbank held sleeping partridge, and how to dig out wood mice in their deep runways when all other food failed. He grew lean and gaunt as a specter, but somehow he survived.

A third week went by and January came, bringing with it a still cold unlike anything Slippy had yet known. He still searched the heights for his friends, and at length one afternoon he sighted a number of white specks against a far-off cliff. A valley lay between, but Slippy, undaunted, descended clear to timber line, bucked the deep drifts, and labored grimly up the other slope. Before nightfall he had come up with the goat band again, whinnying his satisfaction.

January was a terrible month up on the roof of the world. Storm after storm swept the heights. From the forested valleys below the hunger call of wolves and coyotes sounded nightly, and sometimes the whining scream of a cougar would split the breeze. Even the wild goats began to feel the pinch of hunger, for the snows were such that the highest peaks became mantled with white.

Now came the time of greatest peril, when hunting in the valleys grew lean and the mountain lions sought the peaks for meat. The broad pads of these killers held

27

them up on the deep snow where the sharp hoofs of the goats cut through. The deadly stalking of the great cats could not wholly be guarded against, no matter what the craft of the goats. The cougars would prowl the heights until they found some point where the goats would have to pass. Lying in wait for hours until the band approached, the lion would drop like a bolt from some overhanging rock, and one of the band would pay with its life.

After each attack by a lion the goats would take refuge for days among the rim rocks. But they could not remain there indefinitely, and when hunger drove them down again the killers would again hang like a bad conscience to their trail. By the end of January five of the original fifteen goats had been killed, and still there was no break in the weather.

Slippy came through that grim month unscathed, partly because he was always struggling along at the tail end of the file of goats, and partly because the lions were suspicious of him, associating him and his scent with man, their greatest enemy. The old leader of the goats also escaped attack. That hoary patriarch would have welcomed facing a lion in fair combat. But the killers were cowards at heart, and had no stomach for tackling a four-hundred-pound fighting machine, with sinews of whalebone and a hide like a thick wool rug.

As February came and the deep snows still made hunting in the lower forests impossible for the cougars, the contest between the goats and the great cats came to an inevitable dramatic head. For weeks the goats had been growing warier and warier. They never approached a rock cliff without beating carefully up wind, eyes and nostrils alert for a sign of the enemy. For a fortnight there had been no casualties in the band, for they had lived on the leanest fare in order to avoid every possible ambush.

At last, on a still night when a dying moon bathed the white peaks in a spectral light, the lions, driven by unbearable hunger, brought the battle to the old patriarch.

Slippy and Sounder were some five hundred feet below the band this night. All were bedded near the brink of a broad, open ledge, where no enemy could possibly approach without first appearing boldly in the open. It was that hour before the dawn when night hunters that have found no kill turn desperate.

The jagged peaks roundabout leaned toward the morning stars, when an eddy of breeze carried the rank scent of lion to the sensitive nostrils of the old leading goat. He had the band on their feet in an instant. Then, after long minutes of tension, a mountain lion showed among the rocks of the distant cliff, another close behind. This was the pair that had ravaged the peaks all winter. Beyond all caution now, they advanced into the wash of moonlight, red-eyed with hunger.

The goats backed to the brink of the ledge, the old patriarch well to the fore, facing the cliff. Minutes of waiting passed. The lions flattened themselves to the snow, advancing but a few inches at a time, their eyes holding the goats with a murderous fixity. Never before had they carried the war into the open like this. Their every instinct was for waiting and indirection, but fiercer even than their blood lust was the gnaw of hunger. The big muscles of their shoulders bulged above their gaunt, crouched bodies.

Slippy, standing five hundred feet down slope, was trembling faintly, unable to make any other move. Weakened by cold and privation, he wanted only to sink down in the snow; wanted only to creep away and sleep. But the lions came on—so stealthily that they seemed not to move at all, save for their long tails that twitched like snakes. Puffs of icy wind sent sprays of snow across the ledge from the rocks above.

Even old Sounder seemed to have no battle challenge in him this night. For once he made no sound, but merely got to his feet, his hackles rising stiffly along his gaunt shoulders. As yet the lions had not seen him.

Abruptly the foremost lion launched himself forward in an attempt to pass the old leader's guard. But the bulky patriarch, agile as any kid, reared and whirled on his hind legs with a bawl of defiance, and a lightning thrust of his crinkly black horns caught the killer in mid-air. The lion was jerked to one side as if by invisible wires. Almost in the instant he alighted he returned to the attack, in a succession of short rushes and angry snarls. The *wheep-wheep* of his great mailed paws tore patches from the old goat's white coat but, wheeling and pivoting with flashing horns, the leader still managed to block the lion at every turn.

Back to the very brink of the ledge they maneuvered, till another step would have pitched them both into oblivion. Still by a miracle the cougar was unable to break through the guard to the huddled kids and nannies behind.

Then, into the breach, help came flying in a shaggy wolfish form. Old Sounder, who might have crept away unnoticed from that place of death and danger, had

30

hesitated but a brief minute. Straight into the face of the cougar he launched his hundred and fifty pounds. What followed was a storm of tawny arms and legs and flying snow, amid a crescendo of screams and growls and the white flash of fang and claw.

The lion's mate, meanwhile, had been circling the rocks to come in from the opposite side and make a swift kill while the old patriarch was engaged. But no opening offered. Instead, there stood Slippy in her way, a chunky, sorrel-colored horse trembling in every limb but with white teeth bared, hoofs dancing, nostrils ruckling in a frenzy of defiance. Even as Sounder attacked, the lioness sprang from haunches like coiled springs. Slippy moved in the same instant. He pivoted and powerful hind legs shot out, catching the lioness a glancing blow on the shoulder.

With a fiendish squall the big cat struck the snow, then bounded to the pony's back, her four sets of claws sinking deep into his quivering sides. Slippy staggered, pitched to his nose but struggled up again, his wild whinnies of protest blending with the battle cry of the patriarch.

The mailed paw of the lioness crooked beneath Slippy's neck and wrenched cunningly. Her custom was to kill by dislocation. Slippy bucked like a demon. His blunt teeth caught one silky ear of the attacker and ground it into a bleeding rag. The lioness screamed with rage and sprang free—unable, like all cats, to stand pain. She crouched for another spring, perilously close to the lip of the ledge, as Slippy wheeled with a desperate whinny. In that instant old Sounder was beside him.

31

Somehow the dog had broken free of the lion and come to the aid of his friend.

Sounder sprang in with a roar; the lioness struck and sprang aside. Once more, terrible and avenging, Slippy swung around to deliver a broadside kick with his powerful hind legs. It landed squarely and soddenly against the big cat's ribs, flinging her back. She teetered a moment on the very brink, her claws rasping on the ice and snow, and Slippy kicked again. A moment the tawny body dangled over the snowy ledge, then slipped and pitched downward, writhing and screaming, into the gulf below.

The male lion, circling the old goat, turned his head at the death cry of his mate. It was only an instant, but for the patriarch, dancing on his hind legs preparing for a charge, it was enough. He drove in with a mighty thrust of lowered horns that rolled the killer over. Before he found his feet the old goat hit him again like a pile-driver, while from the opposite side old Sounder was closing in to finish the kill.

It was too much for the lion. Before either opponent could reach him again, the killer of the peaks was streaking, belly down, for the shelter of the cliffs.

At that point Slippy and Sounder might have established themselves as masters of the mountain wilderness and all its inhabitants. To them it was an empty glory, however; particularly to old Sounder, wounded far more seriously than he knew. Torn and red and hardly recognizable, he collapsed presently on his side, his blood staining the snow. He gave but a few feeble thumps of his tail when Slippy came and stood above him.

It was two hours before his fevered wounds stopped bleeding. All that day Slippy stayed close to his friend. The goat band, too, hovered near in a strange concern, drawn by the bond that had been established between them in battle.

That victory over the cougars seemed a winning over famine and the winter hardships as well, for at nightfall there came an abrupt break in the weather.

Before morning the snowy slopes were melting in a thousand tiny rivulets and through the silence sounded the occasional long, sucking *chug* of sinking snow. Mountain and forest seemed to relax and breathe again. There might come other freezes, but the worst of the winter was now over.

Meanwhile Sounder was fighting with the last supreme Enemy, and barely holding his own. Somehow Slippy seemed to know. By gentle nudges of his warm, inquiring nose, he kept rousing the old dog from his coma of pain and fever, urging him to follow down the mountain to the ranch house. Again and again through that long day the dog would rally and rise on shaky legs and follow Slippy for a hundred and fifty yards, only to sink down again and rest until strength was renewed.

Night had fallen when they reached the ranch. All was deserted still, but the corrals and pastures were almost free of snow, the warm breeze was like a benison, and the air was filled with the soft chuckle of trickling water. Stretched out on the ranch porch, Sounder let the old familiar scents and sounds slide through his ears and nose. His heart took strength and the shadowy Enemy faded away, defeated.

33

It was about noon next day, as the goat band fed slowly along the snowline above the ranch, that something startled them into sudden flight. Slippy saw them go and flung up his head, then wheeled at another movement and the old familiar sound of human voices.

Jesse Hunnicutt, with Jake Marden and young Jesse behind him, had just rounded a bend in the valley trail, each mounted and leading a pack animal. Releasing their pack horses at sight of Slippy, all three spurred forward with incredulous whoops and yells.

And Slippy? Flinging up his head with a wild whinny, he sprang from complete rest to full speed in a single shutter-click of time. Down the length of the great pasture he thundered to meet his friends, running with all that was in him, his small mountain-hardened legs moving like pistons in perfect rhythm. To the watching men his flying hoofs seemed never to strike the ground.

The riders reined in to gape, sitting their horses as though struck in stone. On he came, until he was eight feet in front of the horsemen. In the final instant before head-on collision, Slippy jerked aside with no slightest slackening of speed, then swept round and round them in great wild circles, whinnying again and again with happiness. The men continued to watch in silent fascination.

Always slimly built and lightly muscled, Slippy was now leaned down to the point of emaciation, the tendons like slender skeins at his wrists and hocks—but skeins of steel. He looked more than ever as if he might drift before the wind.

Jesse Hunnicutt was muttering as he watched. "Look at him, just look at him!" he cried. "There's an antelope and a greyhound rolled up in him—to say nothin' of a cannon ball! And that legwork! And to think I left him for dead!"

They waited till Slippy had worked off some of his steam and joy and come to a stand. Then Jesse Hunnicutt dismounted, while young Jesse spurred toward the ranch house to look for his dog. The rancher was aware of a vague but definite shame as he approached the game little horse. He was guilty, as he saw it now, of rank desertion. Slippy's mane was a gnarled and matted mass from the winter winds; his lean sides were no longer sleek, but woolly as a range horse's—nature's desperate effort to help ward off the cold. The man's eye picked out the wounds along his back.

"Cougars, Boss!" cried Jake Marden. "The pore little cuss! I reckon he saw a thing or two besides cold and hunger up there among the peaks!"

"Well, I'll be John Brown!"

Jesse put a hand on Slippy's sturdy neck, then bent to run exploring, incredulous fingers over the solid chest and hocks and pasterns. He swore soulfully again. Never had he dreamed of seeing a two-year-old in such superb condition. In spite of cougars and cold, winter and hunger, or perhaps because of them, he was looking at a champion.

For a space man and horse stood gazing at each other across the great gulf of silence that hangs forever between the human and animal world. Had Slippy been human the gulf might never have been spanned after what had happened in the fall. But being animal, he bent his head to rub it lovingly against the man's sleeve.

35

It was enough for him that the voices of his human friends once more fell blessedly on his ears.

Up at the ranch house old Sounder too had rubbed away that gulf as if it had never been, and young Jesse was kneeling on the porch steps, his arms full of his old dog.

○ 2 ○

THE MATCH RACE

by WALTER FARLEY

THE DAY of the big race! The eyes of the nation turned upon Chicago. All morning long trains, buses, autos and planes roared into the city discharging thousands of passengers bound for the track.

A carnival spirit swept over the city. Offices closed for the day, and everywhere one question was asked, "Who will win—Cyclone or Sun Raider?"

"How're you doin', Charlie?" asked a motorcycle cop of a policeman who was directing traffic at one of Chicago's busiest corners, as he pulled up beside him.

"Never saw anything like it, Pat!" came the answer. "Where the devil they all coming from?" Horns blew from the endless lines of cars that stretched far down the avenues.

"I'm worn out myself. They're just about packed solid from here to the track. They'll never get all of 'em inside!"

"They're comin' from all over the country to see this race. Boy, I'd like to be up there myself—to see Cyclone lick 'em!"

The motorcycle cop kicked his motor over. "So would

I," he yelled above the roar. "But it's going to be Sun Raider by three lengths!"

"We'll see. Say, what do you think of this mystery horse?"

"Nothin' much—guess everyone's beginning to wonder how he got in the race anyway. He won't figure in it at all—that's inside stuff! See you later. . . ."

In a large apartment house, not far from the track, Alec's mother and his Aunt Bess looked out the large living-room window at the slow-moving traffic below them. In the distance they could see the track already jammed with people.

"Bess, did you ever see such traffic in all your life?" Mrs. Ramsay asked. "What on earth is happening over there?"

"Don't tell me that you haven't heard about the big match race that's being run today. Everyone has been talking about it. Why, I even have tickets—I was going to surprise you!"

"But, Bess, I've never seen a horse race in my life. I won't know what it's all about!"

"There's nothing to it," her sister laughed. "The horse that gets around the track first wins! I don't go myself much, but this is something nobody should miss. For the first and only time Sun Raider and Cyclone are going to meet. You've heard of them. It'll probably be the grandest horse race of all times. And if you think we're not going to see it when we only live a quarter of a mile away from the track, why—" She looked out of the window. "Look at those crowds! Come, Belle, let's get our hats and coats and go so that we'll get seats."

Mrs. Ramsay shook her head as she went for her hat and coat. "If my husband or son ever find out about my seeing this race, I won't have a moment's peace when I get home. I'll have to take that horse of Alec's right into the house! I told you, Bess, how they're both so crazy over him. I have all I can do now to keep everything under control. . . . They'd certainly love to see this race!"

"It is too bad they're not here, but they'll probably listen in on the radio. . . ."

A plane dropped out of the cloudless sky. Swiftly it circled the field and then came roaring down and rolled to a stop.

The passengers hurried toward the door. "Just about time to make it, if we hurry," one of them said.

The stewardess called, "Bus is waiting directly ahead to take you to the track!" The passengers sprinted for the car.

Alec's father darted into a seat behind the driver. "Think we'll get there before they start?" he asked.

"Yeah, I think so. They always take some time getting those temperamental babies on the track!" the driver answered.

"Sun Raider always puts up a terrific fight beforehand anyway," the man who slipped into the seat next to him said. "He's a lot wilder than Cyclone."

"Might as well do his fighting then," said a man behind them. "He won't be anywhere near Cyclone once they're off!"

"Oh, yeah? It'll be Sun Raider by two lengths today!" He turned to Mr. Ramsay. "Who do you think is going to win?" he asked.

"I'm picking the mystery horse."

"Say, don't you know that's a publicity stunt," the man answered. "I'll bet you there won't even be a third horse out there today!"

"We'll see," Alec's father said. "We'll see."

Alec stroked the Black. "It's almost time, fella," he said. The stallion pawed at the floor of his stall. Outside a line of policemen kept the eager spectators away. In the distance Alec could see the stands jammed with people. Band music drifted toward them. Henry came back from looking over the track.

"Fast as the devil," he said. "Better go over and weigh in, son," he said. He stopped and his eyes blinked a little as he put a hand on the green shirt Alec wore. "Fits pretty good, doesn't it?" he smiled.

"Swell," Alec answered. "So do the pants and the cap." He put on the cap and pulled the long peak down over his eyes to show Henry.

Henry straightened the Number 3 on Alec's arm. "They'll bring you luck," he said. "They did me. . . ."

Alec weighed in and was on his way back to the stables when he passed the two jockeys who were riding Cyclone and Sun Raider. They looked much older than the pictures he had seen of them in the newspapers.

One of them saw him. "Say, you're the kid with the mystery horse, aren't you?"

Alec nodded.

"So you're actually going to ride in this race!" Sun Raider's jockey grinned. "We thought you were just part of a publicity gag, didn't we, Dave?"

The other jockey pulled him by the arm. "Come on,"

40

he said, "quit wastin' time." Then he looked at Alec. "Better take it easy in this race, kid." They turned and walked away.

Alec's anger mounted as he walked toward the stables. Who did those guys think they were, anyway! Just because they were old hands at this game they thought they owned the track.

Henry had the Black out of his stall when he got back.

"All set, kid?" he asked.

"All set."

The noise from the distance made the stallion nervous and he chafed at the bit in his mouth. Alec rubbed his neck.

"Just a few things I want you to remember, Alec," Henry continued. "There isn't much to tell you about handling the Black—you know more about him than I do. You're a good rider, and I've taught you all the tricks I know—now, it's up to you to put them in use. Those other two jockeys are the slickest riders in the game. They won't let you get away with a thing—but they won't try anything that's outside the rules; they're smart but not dirty. They're out to win, but so are you. Remember you've got all the horse under you that they have."

"I'm sure of that, Henry," Alec interrupted as he looked proudly at the Black.

"I can't tell you to hold him back," Henry continued, "because you won't be able to. Stay on him and ride like you never have before! If the Black's the kind of a horse we've been figuring him to be, he should win all the way!"

Cyclone was the first out of the barn for the big race. He received lusty cheers on his way to the paddock. He was draped in a flaming red robe and wore red blinkers. His two forelegs were taped.

A few minutes later Sun Raider was led from the barn almost wholly concealed in a white woolen blanket. All four legs were bandaged. He pranced nervously and his small head turned viciously around. Another cheer went up from the crowd gathered around the paddock when they saw him.

Then a hush fell upon the crowd as the Black appeared, covered in his new black robe and accompanied by old Napoleon. Alec held him by the lead rope attached to his bridle. The stallion reared and Alec let the rope slip through his fingers until he came down. The Black's eyes blazed when he saw the other stallions. Alec remembered the fight the Black had had with the chestnut stallion in Rio. He tightened his grip on the rope and walked him far behind the others when they reached the ring.

The silence was broken by a man's loud yell, "There's the mystery horse!" Then everyone started talking. They hadn't expected to see anything like the Black. "He's even bigger than Sun Raider!" Alec heard one man exclaim.

A few minutes later one of the track officials called, "Riders up!"

The blankets were whipped off the horses. Henry saddled the Black and then boosted Alec into the saddle. "Let the others get out first, so there won't be any trouble," he said, as they went slowly around the ring. The Black's gaze was on the horses far ahead of him.

His nostrils quivered and he shook his head nervously. Alec knew that only Napoleon beside him kept him under control.

A long line of policemen kept the crowd back and made a path from the paddock to the track. The bugle sounded. The Black raised his head and his ears pricked forward. Henry led him toward the track.

They stopped at the gate. Cyclone and Sun Raider were already walking past the grandstand on their way to the post. Henry looked up at Alec. "Well, kid, you're on your own now," he said quietly. "Go to it!"

Alec's heart pounded as he saw the solid mass of people stretched out before him. "O.K., Henry," he said. Old Napoleon neighed plaintively as Henry kept him from following the Black out on the track.

Every vantage point in and around the outer fences of the course was jammed with excited fans. Many perched on roof tops fully a mile from the starting point. Their attention was focused on Sun Raider and Cyclone as they passed the stands. Then suddenly they saw a giant black horse, his mane waving like windblown flame, coming down the track. Spectators rose in their seats and excited hands raised glasses to their eyes.

"It's the mystery horse!" shouted a well-known sports commentator to a nation-wide radio audience. One hand left the microphone and picked up the program. "He's listed as the Black and ridden by Alec Ramsay. He's raising quite a commotion around here! He's one of the biggest horses that I've ever seen—if not *the* biggest. He's black, coal black. He's big and strong and doesn't seem to want to go near the other horses. Alec Ramsay on his back is having a very difficult time controlling him. Lord! I've seen plenty of horses in my time, but none with action like that! I'd say that this horse that most of us have labeled 'Neville's Folly' is going to be very much in the picture of this race. Yes, sir, it's shaping up to be the greatest match race of all times or I miss my guess!

"Now he's approaching the starting line. Cyclone doesn't want to go near him and moves away. Sun Raider stands his ground and his teeth are bared. The starter's having quite a time. That black horse is a devil! He wants to fight! They're lining up. There he goes up into the air! He's plunging at Sun Raider, striking! Listen to that black devil scream—never in my life have I heard anything like it! It's risen to such a high pitch that it's practically a whistle—you probably all can hear it! There, Alec Ramsay's got him down—that boy sure can stick on a horse. What a struggle is going on out there, folks! Over eighty thousand people here, and I can say without fear of contradiction, they've never seen anything like this before! Take it from me the Black is a wild stallion—never clearly broken. A savage on the race track!

"You folks who have seen Sun Raider know that they don't come much wilder than he, but he's certainly met his match today—in fighting, anyway! He's backing away from the Black now! They've got Cyclone in between the two of them. That's better. Alec Ramsay is managing the Black now. That boy is doing wonders— I wouldn't be in his shoes for all the money in the world! Sun Raider won't stand still. He's furious—he hates the Black. He's broken out of line. There he goes striking at the Black! He's hit him! Oh, oh, the Black's leg is bleeding—that was a pretty hard blow. Alec Ramsay can't hold his horse any longer—he's on his hind legs and plunging at Sun Raider. There's no way of stopping this thing! Sun Raider is backing up again—he doesn't stand a chance with that black devil! Wait, there's Alec Ramsay pulling on his horse's head—he's turning him off. He's getting him under control again. He's got him on the outside. Sun Raider doesn't want to fight any more. He's back at his position on the pole.

"Looks as though the starter is going to send them off—while he's got them there. The Black's leg is bleeding pretty badly. Sun Raider doesn't seem to be much the worse off for the fight. Alec Ramsay is leaning over looking at the Black's wound. He's getting off—he'll probably leave the race, too bad——*They're off!* The starter wasn't watching Alec Ramsay—he was climbing out of his saddle.

"Cyclone and Sun Raider are fighting head and head as they flash past the stands. The Black is left at the post; he's out of the race. No, no, here he comes after them! His jockey is only half in the saddle. Now he's on! He's trying desperately to pull the Black to a stop; he doesn't want him to run with his leg in that condition. He's pulling furiously on the reins, but it doesn't seem to be doing any good. The Black wants to run—he's fighting for his head! He's almost pulling Alec Ramsay straight up in his saddle. Now he's ripped the reins out of his hands! He's close to a hundred yards behind, too far to catch up—but he's going to run!

"Cyclone has beaten Sun Raider to the first turn— they're both running under the whip. Each wants to set the pace! Cyclone's jockey is deliberately pulling his

45

horse up, so that Cyclone's churning hind quarters are right in Sun Raider's nose. That's a shrewd move as it gives his mount a breather after that stretch sprint and forces Sun Raider to check his speed from running on Cyclone's heels!

"But now as they round the turn, Sun Raider, the California comet, is moving up alongside Cyclone, and as they enter the backstretch they're running neck and neck——"

Suddenly a deafening roar rose from the stands. "Look, look," yelled the commentator hysterically. "The Black is coming up like a house on fire! You've never in your life seen a horse run like this! He's all power—all beauty. The distance between him and the others is lessening. How it's lessening! I wouldn't believe it if I wasn't seeing it with my own eyes. The Black is running the others down! Cyclone and Sun Raider are fighting for the lead going into the last turn. The Black's almost behind them. What action! What a tremendous stride! The crowd is going crazy. Sun Raider is passing Cyclone on the turn and going into the lead! Here they come down the homestretch——"

The crowd began to scream as the fighting horses came thundering toward them. Sun Raider was surging ahead. Cyclone was falling back—the Black had him! Sun Raider was two lengths in front, his jockey batting away with his whip. The Black started moving up. Now he was a length behind. No whip was being used on him —his jockey was like a small burr lost in the stallion's thick, black mane.

Hysteria swept the crowd as the horses passed them for the second time—the finish line only one hundred

Into the lead the Black swept

yards away. "He'll never get Sun Raider!" yelled the radio announcer. The stallion flashed by the stands going faster with every magnificent stride. With a sudden spurt he bore down on Sun Raider. For a moment he hesitated as he came alongside. The crowd gasped as the Black's ears went back and his teeth bared. There was a movement on his back; his jockey's hand rose and fell on the stallion's rear quarters for the first time in the race. Into the lead the Black swept, past the cheering thousands—a step, a length, two lengths ahead—then the mighty giant plunged under the wire.

The Black rounded the first turn and had entered the backstretch again before Alec was able to slow him down. He knew that only the pain in the stallion's leg enabled him to do it. Finally he brought him to a stop.

Alec forgot the cheering thousands as he slid, exhausted, from the stallion's back. He bent down to look at the wound. There was so much blood! Alec took his handkerchief and wrapped it around the Black's leg to try to stop the bleeding. "You shouldn't have done it, Boy," he said.

A station wagon roared around the track toward them, leaving a cloud of dust in its wake. The Black reared as it pulled up to them. Henry jumped out and pulled a man behind him.

"Is he hurt much?" he asked Alec anxiously. "Here's the veterinary——"

"Can't tell. It's bleeding pretty bad and I know it's hurting him."

The veterinary bent down to examine the wound. Henry went to the wagon and returned carrying a pail of water, sponge and bandage. The veterinary cut off Alec's handkerchief that was now covered with blood.

The voices of the clamoring thousands stilled, as they realized what was happening on the track. All eyes were upon the small group.

The veterinary straightened up. "He's lost a lot of blood, but he has a leg like iron," he said. "Give him a couple of months' rest and he'll be as good as new!"

Alec and Henry looked at each other and their eyes were moist. No word was spoken while the veterinary bandaged the Black's leg. Then Henry broke the silence. "Well, Alec," he said, "guess you and the Black did it!"

The veterinary stood up. "O.K.," he said. "And now I think they're waiting for you over at the winner's circle."

As Henry boosted the boy into the saddle, an avalanche of cheers rose from the crowd. The stallion's ears pricked forward and he looked wildly around. Alec patted him on the neck. For the first time he realized that the race was over, that they had won. "You did it, Boy," he said proudly. "You did it!" The blood raced through his veins and his heart pounded against his ribs as the crowd cheered them on their way back. The stallion reared as they approached the grandstand.

Thousands of pairs of eyes watched the Black as he pranced out there beyond the crowd. He did not want to come closer. Yet he did not seem to fight his rider. Some of the crowd broke through the police line and rushed toward him. They stopped suddenly when he reared, and moved back quickly as he came toward them, head and tail erect. His action was beautiful, springy, and every few steps he jumped with marvelous ease and swiftness. Experts shook their heads knowingly at the Black's performance. "Here," said one old man, "is the greatest piece of horseflesh that ever set foot on any track!"

Alec rode the Black up to the judge's stand, and into the winner's circle. The stallion stood still for the first time. Alec and Henry could hardly believe their eyes. Even flashlight bulbs exploding close at hand only caused him to toss his head. They put the horseshoe of roses around his neck.

°3°

KING OF THE RANGE

by MARGARET JAMISON

HAL FELT young and inexperienced. He was glad to be included in the hunt for wild horses, but he had never been so far from the ranch before. Ned and Sandy, the two older boys from Circle R Ranch, had been "mustangers" for several years now. They knew the right method of "walking down" the wild horses by cutting across their path and circling them. Then the animals could be rounded up and driven to the ranch corral.

As the three boys tied up their horses on a wooded slope and began making camp for the night, Hal looked enviously at Ned's new sisal hemp lasso. *He* wanted a rope, too. They were expensive, though. His father, foreman of Circle R Ranch, said he must wait till he was older. Sometimes Hal borrowed a rope and practiced on calves out in the pasture.

After the boys had eaten their camp supper, Ned called to Hal, "Hey, Baby, come over here to this open space and watch a real roper practice." Hal wished Ned wouldn't tease him about his roping, or call him "Baby."

Just then the ranch ponies tethered near began to whinny restlessly. A sound like thunder came from the

level flatlands west of camp. Hal recognized it as hoofbeats. Then a long shriek split the air.

"What's that?" Hal asked, his heart pounding.

"It's Viento," Ned answered. "I heard him once before
when I was riding fence for Mr. Brown."

Hal tensed with excitement. Viento! The great mustang stallion, called by the Spanish word for wind because he ran so fast! Hal thrilled at the thought of being
so near the swift, brave leader of all the wild horses for
many miles around. He had heard of Viento.

Who hadn't, in that section of the country? Mustangs,
descendants of horses brought to America by Spanish
explorers, roamed the saw-tooth hills below the Rockies.
They made excellent ranch horses, once they were
caught and tamed.

But Viento was different. He was the boldest outlaw
and the proudest thief of all the untamed rovers. Like a
red-brown streak, his long black mane and tail streaming
in the wind, he would rush up to a herd of tame ranch
horses. Nipping and kicking, he would separate the
mares and colts that he wanted for his own herds. Then
he would drive the quarry off to his lonely hill fortress
somewhere up among the windy peaks.

No mustanger ever had been able to come within a
half mile of Viento. As a long-legged colt he had seen
his mother captured and led off with a rope on her proud
neck, her beautiful head to the ground. Afterwards,
Viento had become a threat to all ranchers in North
Texas. He was more intelligent than most horses, and
braver than most, and as long as he was free ranch herds
were not safe. Like the wind for which he was named, he
was a law unto himself.

Ned twirled his new rope in circles and loops. Then Ned chuckled, "I'm glad Viento's back. Tell you a secret, fellas. I plan to win that prize of two longhorns Mr. Brown offers to the mustanger who ropes Viento."

"Huh!" Sandy snorted. "Grown men have trailed Viento for weeks, trying to cut him off from grass and water so he could be captured. Last year he led five men from Bar 6 Ranch clear up into Oklahoma Territory. And *you* expect to rope him!"

"Why not?" Ned asked. "I've studied his habits since I was knee-high to a cricket. Tonight he's probably headed for the Wilderness River canyon with his herd. Mustangs never sleep till early in the morning. Then I'll bet I can sneak up on him in the canyon.

"Tomorrow before daylight, Baby and I will go to the chute that leads into the canyon of Wilderness River. You, Sandy, will go farther up the river to where Red Rock Creek runs into it. You can head Viento off if he goes that way."

"Okay, boss," Sandy drawled.

Hal was too wakeful to sleep when the boys unrolled their blankets to bed down near the fire. Several times he thought he heard a long, shrill horse's neigh and the beat of hoofs in the distance, stamping their challenge.

It seemed but a minute later that Ned shook him awake urgently. "Come on, sleepy-head! Sandy's gone already—I saddled your horse. Let's get started while the moon is still up."

Quickly Hal put on his high-heeled, sharp-pointed cowboy boots, got on his pony, and followed Ned's horse out to the damp grass that edged the Wilderness River flats. The early morning was moonlit and cool, with little wind blowing. At last, far ahead, the boys glimpsed a wide, moving, dark shape.

"Sh! It's Viento's band," Ned whispered over his shoulder. "Go slow so they can't get a scent of us."

Hal smiled and his eyes grew big. Viento himself must be close by.

At last the boys reached a grove of live oaks above the canyon. There they tied their horses, dismounted, and crept along a grassy chute that led down to Wilderness River between steep slopes of rock. Neighs and squeals of horse stock came to their ears. When they reached the river bed an unearthly sound broke loose.

"That's Viento's call of warning to his herd," Ned said softly.

Hal shivered as the weird cry echoed and re-echoed in the canyon. He wanted to turn and run. But he knew that if he did Ned would never let up teasing him. If he could only see Viento! He peered up the slope beyond him. The moon had gone. It was almost daylight. Something, he couldn't be sure what, was climbing the rocky expanse above. Quickly he nudged Ned and pointed.

"It's Viento," Ned shouted. "We're blocking his way out by the chute, and the river bank is impassable here on account of the big rocks. He's trying to find some other trail out of the canyon."

Now they could see the big mustang picking his way carefully up the steep slope. A patch of sunlight fell on his smooth red-brown coat. Hal could see the horse's steel-tense muscles quivering with effort, could see his perfect body poised for a moment in his ascent. "Look at him!" Hal breathed. "He's like a bronze statue!"

By then the horse had reached a long, narrow shelf that jutted out over the canyon and fell in a drop of several hundred feet to the river bed. Above the shelf stretched a high tower of smooth cap-rock, which curved down and formed a barrier at one end of the shelf.

"He's trapped unless he can jump across the river!" Ned shouted. "I'd say the width is about eighteen feet at this part of the canyon. Well, here goes after him. I've got to win those two steers from Mr. Brown."

No sooner had Ned spoken than his high boot heel slipped on a rock and he fell to the ground. "Ouch!" he yelled. "I've twisted my ankle. No climbing for me now!"

"I'm sorry, Ned!" Hal bent over his groaning companion. Ned ruefully eyed the narrow ledge where the two of them could see Viento racing back and forth, his black mane tossing. Suddenly a thought popped into Hal's mind. Here was a chance to prove to Ned that he, Hal, was no "baby," and that he, too, could use a rope.

"Ned, if you'll lend me your lasso, I'll go up and try to rope Viento."

"You?" Ned's doubting laugh resounded in the canyon.

"I mean it. Will you lend me your rope?" Hal asked, his eyes serious.

"Of course, Baby," Ned replied, placing the smooth yellow coils in the younger boy's hand.

Five minutes later Hal was halfway up the slope. After that the going got harder. Once he came near slipping.

"Careful, Sonny," Ned cautioned.

Hardly noting Ned's new name for him, Hal kept climbing. Now he could see Viento watching him from above, large brown eyes fixed on the dread coil of rope

across the boy's shoulder. Just as Hal stepped up onto
the ledge Viento wheeled and rushed to the open end
where it jutted above the river. There he stopped, pawing the ground.

Hal's hand trembled. What if Viento should charge
him?

"Rope him, mustanger!" Ned shouted up to him.

Hal grinned. Mustanger, Ned had called him. Then
Hal was no longer a baby, but a mustanger, with the
king of all mustangs just beyond rope length. He stepped
forward and began to twirl the rope to gain momentum.
With one quick motion he let the coils fly. They whizzed
through the air, straightened as the noose caught around
Viento's right foreleg and held.

Suddenly Hal's fingers burned. The rope! It was being
pulled out of his hand! It was gone! In amazement, he
watched Viento pause for a moment, then vault into
space, the free rope-end dangling behind him. Like that
of a winged horse, the mustang's graceful body seemed
to hang in the air. Then his front hoofs hit the ground
on the opposite side of the canyon. His rear legs pushed
mightily to obtain a hold.

Hal held his breath. If Viento fell to the river bed far
below—. But no, the horse was on his feet again, unhurt.
With a defiant toss of his head he galloped off.

Hal laughed in pure relief. He was glad, glad Viento
had escaped. Such a beautiful, brave animal should be
free.

"Did you see that, Ned?" he called to the figure sitting
down beneath.

"I did," Ned replied heartily. "Never knew a horse
could fly! Twenty feet at least, he jumped."

"But—I forgot for a minute—your new rope! It's gone, Ned." What would Hal's father say when he heard about this, he wondered.

"Come on down. We'll worry about the rope later," Ned said, getting up and testing his ankle gingerly. Soon the two boys were riding across the flats toward camp. Few words passed between them. Ned might be angry with him for losing the new rope, Hal thought. Not only that, but would Viento tangle himself up in the rope and get hurt?

As the two boys neared camp a deep voice called, "Hello, mustangers. How are you getting along?" Hal's father, Sandy, and Mr. Brown came out of the thicket to meet them. The men explained that they had ridden out to see how things were going.

Ned made a wry face as he dismounted from his horse. Then with a chuckle he said, "Hal won your prize of two steers, Mr. Brown. He roped Viento."

"Roped Viento?" the others chorused. They looked at Hal in amazement, almost in disbelief.

Hal stood speechless, hardly believing his ears. He hadn't liked Ned's teasing nickname for him. He had almost disliked Ned. Now Ned was trying to give him the prize! His face flamed, and a lump came into his throat.

Just then Sandy pushed forward, a lasso in his hand. "Isn't this your rope, Ned?" he asked. "I found it below Wilderness flats on my way back to camp."

Ned shook his head and said, "No, it *was* my rope, but it's Hal's now. He needs one, and he roped Viento with it."

Hal and Ned looked at each other and laughed, shar-

ing their secret. Viento had managed to get the troublesome rope off his leg. Maybe he had scraped it off, or
pulled it loose with his sharp teeth.

Briefly Ned described to the others what had happened. When he finished, Mr. Brown boomed, "You win
the prize, Hal. Now you can begin to stock your own
herd of cattle and be a real ranchman. As for Viento, I
doubt if he will dare to steal our ranch horses again
after once feeling a rope on him. He's had his lesson."

Hal's father patted him on the back and said, "Mother
will be proud of you, son. And I'm going to give you a
new rope, the best I can get from the ship-chandler down
in Galveston. Ned can keep his rope. After all, it's the
only one that ever touched Viento." He winked, and
Hal knew that his father, too, was glad the brave stallion
had escaped.

The lump in Hal's throat melted away, and a happy
feeling rose there instead. He felt like whooping, singing, yelling "Hurray!" Viento was free to go his own
swift way, still monarch of the unfenced range and the
lonely hills. Ned and Hal would have good ropes. And
now Hal had a good start toward being a rancher.

But there was still something to be settled for Ned,
who would have given Hal his valuable rope. Turning to
Mr. Brown, Hal said slowly, "Could Ned have one of the
two steers you are giving me for a prize?"

The rancher shook his head but his eyes twinkled as
he replied, "No, Hal, I'm afraid Ned will have to get
along with his own two steers the best way be can."

"But Ned hasn't any steers," Hal protested. "Sandy
has one, but Ned hasn't any. That's why—"

"Yes, Ned has two steers," Mr. Brown interrupted.

"You boys have forgotten what I said about winning the prize. I said I would give two steers to the fellow who could get *his* rope on Viento. It was Ned's lasso that you used, Hal, to rope Viento, but *you* did the roping. So you win two steers, and Ned wins two steers. Now don't you boys try to argue with me about it."

∘4∘

THE ROYAL GREENS

by RUSSELL GORDON CARTER

O N A COOL misty autumn morning in the year 1777, as David Wethervale led the small black mare from the stable, his father said to him, "After today I reckon you'll have to go to school afoot."

David's hand tightened on the bridle, and he swallowed hard. He said, "Then—you have at last found a buyer for her?"

"Aye," Seth Wethervale replied. "A man from over Danbury way is coming tomorrow. I'm sorry, lad, for your sake."

David made no comment, knowing the futility of further pleas and arguments. His father had made up his mind to sell the mare almost a year earlier, soon after Uncle Charles had died from wounds at the hands of Johnson's Tories in York State, leaving the horse to his brother-in-law. At that time Seth Wethervale had said, "She's too light for farm work. I'll have to sell her."

As David rode slowly westward toward the schoolhouse at the Corners, some three miles distant, he was miserable. No one knew the full depths of his feelings for the little mare that had enabled his uncle to carry dispatches for Washington's army. "Hobgoblin," she was named, because of her swift ambling gait and her curious facial markings—a generous spattering of little white flecks that gave her a strange and frightening look. Yet, in spite of name and appearance, she was one of the gentlest horses in western Connecticut. And now, after almost a year of wonderful comradeship, he was about to lose her! It made David feel completely miserable.

Halfway to school, as they were crossing the old wooden bridge over the swift waters of Dog Creek, one of the rotten planks gave way under Hobgoblin's weight, and she stumbled and pitched her rider sidewise into the stream. David scrambled out, breathless and shaken, his hose and breeches dripping. Hobgoblin gazed at him wonderingly, then began to nuzzle at his shoulder. Her manner seemed regretful and apologetic.

David threw an arm impulsively over her drooping neck. " 'Twasn't your fault," he said. " 'Twas that rotten plank. Lucky you didn't break a leg!"

He removed his shoes and proceeded as best he could to squeeze the water out of his clammy breeches. Half an hour passed before he mounted again.

School was in session when David tethered the mare in a pine grove across the road. As he entered the small square building, Mr. Verrill, the schoolmaster, frowned and tightened his thin lips.

"What made you late?" he demanded. "Did you dawdle?"

"No, sir, I pitched off my horse," David replied. "She went through a plank in the bridge, and I landed in the water."

Several of the smaller girls tittered.

Mr. Verrill glowered at them, and the sound subsided at once. "Take your seat," he said to the boy.

After David had sat down between Mary Jacobus and Joseph Trumbull, the schoolmaster reopened the brown-covered speller on his desk and proceeded to call upon the pupils at the front of the room. But David's mind was not on the lesson. He was thinking of Hobgoblin, wondering miserably what would become of her. Would the man from over Danbury way treat her kindly? Would he put her to heavy work?

"David! Stand up and spell 'independent.'"

Joseph Trumbull's elbow against his ribs roused David to the realization that the schoolmaster had called on him. He got slowly to his feet. What was the word Mr. Verrill had asked him to spell? He heard Mary Jacobus whisper something.

"Indignant," he began. "I-n-"

"The word was 'independent!'" Mr. Verrill broke in sharply.

David's thoughts cleared. "Oh, yes, sir. Independent. I-n-d-e-p-e-n-d-a-n-t."

"Wrong!" cried the master. "Who can spell it correctly?"

The schoolroom buzzed with eager voices.

"Now try it again, David."

The boy wrinkled his forehead. Even amid the buzz of eager voices his thoughts had again strayed to the mare. He began uncertainly. "I-n-d-i-g-"

Mr. Verrill sprang from his chair, his face flushed. Seizing his birchwood ruler, he motioned with it to a corner. "Stand over yonder with your face to the wall!" he ordered. "Maybe 'twill help you gather your wits."

David was ashamed of himself. Yet even now, as the lesson resumed, he was unable to give his full attention to it. As he shifted uncomfortably from one foot to the other, his thoughts were once more for Hobgoblin. If only there were something he could do to make his father change his mind.

Half an hour dragged past. With head against the wall, David was listening to Mary Jacobus trying to spell "beatific," when she suddenly uttered a startled exclamation and then began to laugh. Glancing sidewise, he saw a surprising sight. Through the open window close to Mary protruded Hobgoblin's white-flecked head, her ears twitching, her jaws gently chewing a wisp of grass that hung from her lips. Others began to laugh, but a sharp crack of the ruler on the desk brought sudden silence in the schoolroom.

"David!"

"Yes, sir?"

"Why did you not tie up your horse?"

"I—I did, sir."

"It does not look so!"

"She must have freed herself, sir."

"Well, go and tie her up again! You and your horse are a vexation!"

David hurried outside. He thought he had tied the bridle rein securely enough to a young pine, but here it was hanging free. Gathering it up, he led the horse away from the schoolhouse—not back to the pine grove, however, but up the hill to where a solitary apple tree stood above grass that was still long and green.

"There now," he said as he secured the rein to a limb. "You can graze here all you please."

66

He lingered, caressing Hobgoblin's smooth neck and letting her nibble playfully at his shoulder. Must he leave her and return to the schoolroom? With a renewed sense of misery, he allowed his gaze to wander far off. To the east he could see the clustered houses of the village and, to the north of it, the round powder-house built of field stones. Close by stood Amos Thatcher's big barn, which now held all the supplies for the militia. His own house lay out of sight in a valley beyond the town. His gaze lowered to the road winding among patches of woodland, dropping to Dog Creek, then gradually twisting upward toward the Corners.

Suddenly he stiffened and caught his breath. There on the road a quarter of a mile from the Corners a body of men were marching—men with muskets, upwards of two score of them and all clad in dusty green uniforms! He stared with mouth agape, almost unable to believe his eyes. Men in green uniforms marching toward the town!

His throat went abruptly dry as the explanation leaped to his mind. Tories! A detachment of the Royal Greens, Johnson's Tories, who had fatally wounded his uncle a year earlier! They must have come up the old logging road that joined the main road some two hundred yards below the Corners. Now they were doubtless on their way to destroy the militia supplies while the men-folks were at work in the fields!

David jerked the bridle free from round the limb. A moment later his leg was across the gray blanket that served as saddle, and he was on his way down the slope, circling toward the west in order not to be seen from the road.

67

Mr. Verrill, ruler in hand, was at the door when the boy reached the schoolhouse.

"What is the meaning of this?" he demanded. "I told you—"

"There's a party of Royal Greens down yonder on the road!" David interrupted him breathlessly. "They aim to raid the town—"

"Eh, what? I say—here, now! David, where ye goin'—" The schoolmaster's voice trailed off into a blur of sound as horse and rider went quartering down across the field.

Reaching the main road, David drew rein and held Hobgoblin to a slow walk. He knew exactly what he would do. Just beyond Dog Creek a second logging road joined the main road from the north. He would follow the raiding party at a safe distance until he was across the bridge, then he would strike northward up the logging road till he came to open country and then rush eastward as fast as possible. He was sure he could reach the town in time to give the alarm.

David was riding now through an old beech wood, the mare's hoofs making hardly a sound on the soft earth at the right of the road. Ahead of him he could hear Dog Creek tumbling over its stony bed as it raced southward to join a branch of the Housatonic. The sound grew louder as he approached the base of the valley. Overhead a pair of crows called raucously.

Just ahead of him the road turned to the right before it dropped steeply to the creek. David drew rein and listened, but heard nothing except the roaring of the creek and the calling of the crows. Probably the raiders were by now already across the bridge. He urged the horse round the turn and then jerked her to a sudden

68

halt, his heart almost in his throat. Less than fifty yards in front, on the near side of the bridge, marched the raiders! Several in the rear glanced backward and, spying him, called to those ahead.

For an instant David sat rigid, viewing the collapse of his careful plan. He could never reach the north logging road now, and if he were to turn back, the surprise of the town would be complete. The thought was intolerable! Acting on swift impulse, he clapped both heels to the mare's flanks, and away she went straight down the incline.

The suddenness of his charge took the Tories unawares. He saw green-clad figures drawing hurriedly apart in front of him. The wind sang in his ears. The woods rang with the clatter of hoofs and the shouts of men as Hobgoblin thundered downward, her haunches straining, her mane flying, sparks leaping outward from beneath her pounding feet. Something slashed at him as he bent low over her neck. A musket butt glanced off his shoulder. Another swished through the air and struck the mare's haunch, causing her to leap sidewise. A branch raked his face as he swung her back in the middle of the road again.

Only one man was between him and the bridge! He saw the fellow raise his musket threateningly, but before he could fire, Hobgoblin struck him with her shoulder, sending him spinning. The bridge now was only a score of yards distant and seemed to David to be rushing at him at wild breakneck speed. In a terrified instant he pictured what would happen if one of Hobgoblin's feet should go through the hole. Then he steeled himself. He had taught her to jump. She must jump now—for her life! Almost at the edge of the bridge he tightened his legs under her and let his weight fall backward. "Now, girl, now!"

Hobgoblin responded beautifully, landing almost in the center of the bridge. Then she was thundering up the slope beyond. Two or three musket shots rang out as she reached the first turn, and he heard the bullets snap overhead. A moment later horse and rider were round the turn—safe!

But there was no time to waste. David dug his heels against the mare's flanks, urged her to her utmost. When they reached the first house on the outskirts of the town, she was wet and glistening.

A woman appeared in the doorway, wide-eyed.

"Tories!" David shouted, slowing down. "A big band of them on the road!"

Through the heart of the town he clattered, shouting the warning on all sides: "Tories! Two score of the Royal Greens!" Then he made off across the fields where he saw men working.

"Tories!" he shouted. "They're on their way up the west road!"

Somewhere in the town a bugle blared, the uncertain notes quivering across the countryside. On a rise of ground David brought the mare to a halt. He had done his best. From all directions, from the woods to the north and the fields to the east and south and west, men in shirt sleeves were running toward the town—sun-browned, resolute men with scythes or axes in their hands. He saw the first arrivals enter Amos Thatcher's barn, saw them emerge with muskets and powder horns. Others joined them, and as they formed ranks, he caught sight of his father.

It was only when David saw the hastily formed column moving off down the road to the west that he realized the full significance of what was happening. There would be a battle. Men would die, his father, perhaps. He felt suddenly faint. Slipping from Hobgoblin's back, he led her to a gulley and sat down heavily on a rock.

How long he sat there he never was able to determine. From the west came the sound of firing, first a volley, then a second volley, then scattered shots at long intervals, then silence. The faint odor of burnt powder presently touched his nostrils. He stood up, then sat down again. He was cold, too cold to sit still.

He rose to his feet once more and, clutching Hobgoblin's bridle, made his way slowly to the town. Women and young children gathered bewilderingly about him, and he tried as best he could to answer their excited questions. Finally one of the women said, "Let him be now. He's overwrought. Sit ye down here on the step, David, whilst I go and warm some milk for ye."

It was not until well past noon that the militiamen began to return. David saw them come straggling up the hill, and in one group, to his profound relief, he spied his father.

Seth Wethervale came forward at a quick walk. His face was powder-stained.

David ran to meet him. "The Tories—" he began.

"They're in York State by now, them as is left," his father replied grimly. Then his rough hand reached forth and clutched his son's shoulder.

71

"Lad, I be proud o' ye!" he said. "What ye done an' all—"

David smiled and shook his head. " 'Twas Hobgoblin," he protested.

Seth Wethervale nodded. "I know all about it! Mr. Verrill told how you rode headlong down the road right through the midst o' them—"

" 'Twas Hobgoblin," David repeated.

For a long moment father and son looked full at each other—a moment vibrant with understanding.

Finally Seth Wethervale said, "I reckon ye're right. The mare shares the credit." Then he added in a tone meant to be matter-of-fact, "And I reckon, after what's happened, 'twould be a mite unfair to part the two o' ye."

David felt the warm blood come flooding into his face. "You—you mean you'll not sell her after all?"

"Aye, lad, that is what I mean. You've earned the keep of her."

David stared with eyes bright and lips parted, too deeply moved to speak. With a boisterous shout, he suddenly whirled and ran to where Hobgoblin was patiently waiting. A moment later his arm was across her neck and her soft lips were against his shoulder as he told her the joyous news.

∘ 5 ∘

"THE SQUEAK OF LEATHER"

by WILL JAMES

TWENTY FEET of rope is laying between the cowboy's hand and the pony's head. The cowboy is standing there just watching and smiling some at the surprised look that's in the pony's face, that pony had just been stopped sudden in his bucking with an empty saddle;— it was the first time a saddle had been on his slick back and it was no wonder he tried to get out from under that thing; nothing had ever clung there before.

"Now, you just take it easy for a spell, and keep your head up," says that cowboy as he started walking towards the pony.—Legs wide apart, a wild look in his eyes, and a snorting his surprise Smoky watched him come; he didn't know whether to stand his ground and start fighting or back away as the cowboy came.—On he came, and as Smoky was seeing no sign of harm, he stood in his tracks, watched, and waited. A hand touched him on the forehead and moved on down his neck, the cowboy was a talking to him the while, and pretty soon Smoky's heart wasn't thumping so hard no more.——

73

He was then led a little ways, and as he heard the squeak of leather and felt the weight of the saddle with each step he took, an awful hankering came to him to put his head down and try to buck it off, but the cowboy was right there in front of him and he didn't want to be stopped again and so sudden as he'd been stopped that first time.

The other side of the corral was reached and there Clint turned and rubbed Smoky on the ear. "Well, old boy, let's see how you're going to behave when I get up in the middle of you."

Smoky watched the man reach for the latigo and felt the cinch tighten up; a hump came in his back and which made the saddle set near on end,—it was the hump that carried the punch in the buck, and most likely Clint could of led the pony around some till the hump wore down and his back straightened up again, but that rider wasn't for taking the buck out of a bronc too quick. He believed a good sensible horse should buck at the first few "settings" and he wasn't the kind of rider that'd smother that natural feeling and have it come out later, when the horse is supposed to be broke gentle.

He let the hump be and never moved the pony out of his tracks;—he knowed that just one move would be enough to start that pony to exploding, and Smoky was set and just a waiting for that signal to start. He watched the cowboy raise his chaps so the belt wouldn't hinder his leg action, watched him pull his hat brim down solid, and then he couldn't watch no more. Something had come between him and his vision, it was the cowboy's thumb which had layed over his left eyelid and pulled it down over his eye— In the next second he felt a weight added on to that of the saddle, and all of a sudden he could see again.

But what he did see left him starry eyed and paralyzed. For half a minute he just stood like petrified. That cowboy had disappeared from the side of him, and instead, there he was right in the middle of his back and on that hunk of leather he'd been hankering to shed off ever since it was put on there.

Instinct pointed out only one way for him to act,—it was telling him that neither the human nor the leather belonged up there in the middle of him that way, and that if he tried he could most likely get rid of 'em. There was nothing else to do that he could see, and right then he felt that he sure must do *something*.

His head went down, and a beller came out of him that said much as "I want you"— Up went Smoky's withers followed by the hump that made the saddle twist like on a pivot, and last came steel muscles like shot out of the earth, and which carried the whole mixed up and crooked conglomeration of man and horse up in mid air and seemed like to shake there for a spell before coming down. All seemed heads and tails and made a picture of the kind that was mighty hard to see, and still harder to figger out.

Saddle strings was a popping like on a whip lash, leather was a squeaking, corrals shook as the hard hitting hoofs of the pony hit the earth, and a dust was stirred that looked like a young cloud. Smoky was scared, mad, and desperate. All the action, strength, and endurance that was in him was brought out to do its best. Not a hair on his hide was laying idle thru the performance,—

75

every muscle tightened and loosened in a way to shake the weight on his back and make it pop.

Clint felt the muscles work even thru the saddle, and every part of that pony which his legs touched seemed as hard as steel and full of fast working bumps which came and went, twisted his saddle under him, and made him wonder if it was going to stay. It seemed like sometimes that Smoky was headed one way and his saddle another,—he wasn't always sure of the whereabouts of that pony's head; and in all his riding that's what he wanted to keep track of most, cause losing track of a horse's head at them times is something like riding blindfolded—a rider would prepare for one kind of a jolt and meet another, which would cause things to scatter considerable.

Clint was still straight up and on top when Smoky's hard jumps finally dwindled down to crowhops and then a stop. That pony was needing wind mighty bad, and as his nostrils opened wide, was taking in the necessary air, he felt a hand a rubbing along his neck, and wild eyed, ears cocked back at the cowboy that was still there, he stood and heard him talk.

"You done a mighty fine job, little horse," says Clint, "and I'd been disappointed a lot not to've found that kind of spirit in a horse like you."

If Smoky had been raised amongst humans like a dog and been with 'em steady that way, he'd of had a hunch or felt what Clint said and meant. But Smoky was a wild horse of the flats and mountains, and even tho the sound of Clint's tone and the feel of his hand soothed him some, he would buck again and again. It was his instinct to fight the human, and he would fight till that human showed he could handle him and proved a friend.

That had to be done gradual, and Smoky had no way to know as yet that man could be a friend of his, not while the breaking was going on anyway, for thru that spell a horse is *made* to do things he sometimes don't want to do, and which all keeps down the confidence that would come faster if that didn't have to be done.

Smoky was doing some tall figgering as he stood there trembling and wondering if there wasn't something that he could get by with. He'd been made to do things just as that cowboy pleased and he'd found no say in the goings on, none at all. If he could only've bucked him off that would of pleased him a lot, but the little horse didn't know he was on this earth for the purpose of the human and that if he did throw one man another would climb him till finally he'd have to give in and go thru a lot of grief the while.

Smoky felt a light slap on his neck. "Come on, young feller," says the cowboy. "Let's see you trot around the corral a while."

But Smoky bucked more than he trotted. The cowboy let him, and when his head would come up he'd keep him on the go till finally there seemed to be no buck in the horse at all.

"I reckon that'll be enough for you to-day" says Clint as he headed Smoky for the side of the corral and made him face the bars to a stop. He then reached for the pony's left ear and twisted it some, just enough to keep that pony's attention on the twist of that ear most while he got off.——

Clint touched the ground with his right foot, and

keeping his left in the stirrup, at the same time keeping close to the horse's shoulder and out of the reach of his hind feet, he held that position for a few seconds. Smoky was watching him, shaking like a leaf and ready to paw the daylight out of the cowboy at the first wrong move or sudden jab of a knee.

Clint *wanted* him to watch. This was part of the eddication, and all that cowboy wanted to teach right then was for Smoky to stand and not to go to acting up. Slow and easy, at the same time having complete control of himself and his horse, Clint raised himself up in the saddle again. It was done in a way that only bronc busters know. Smoky never even felt the pull on the saddle as the cowboy climbed on, and if that saddle hadn't even been cinched it wouldn't of budged then, so neat it was done.

Clint climbed on and off a few times that way, Smoky stood and shivered, scared, but willing it seemed like to take his medicine. Maybe it'd come to his mind that there was no use fighting that cowboy, or else he was getting tired—anyway that was the last of it; Smoky felt the cinch loosen and then slow and easy the saddle was pulled off. About that time he whirled and faced the rider who was holding the saddle, he took a sniff at the hunk of leather and snorted like to say "Gee! I thought that thing was on me for good."

The saddle was set to one side and the cowboy begin rubbing Smoky's back with a gunny sack, and according to the way that pony acted that felt mighty good, his upper lip stuck out and twitched with every motion of the rubbing, and when Clint finally quit, the little horse's action showed plain that he should do it some more; Clint rubbed again.

"I'm afraid," he says as he grinned and rubbed, "that I'm naturally going to spoil you. Here we just got thru with the first saddling and you're beginning to look for favors already."

Smoky's picket grounds was moved to a fresh one for that night and where the grass was tall, a plenty and green,—but somehow his appetite wasn't at its best, and when the break of day come there was very little sign (as Clint noticed) that the pony had et at all. He'd just stood in one spot, looked like, and seemed to've done tall wondering and figgering instead of feeding. He was ganted up the same as if he'd been rode all that night, and still there was no show of any appetite for the feed that was under and all around him.

As Clint worked in the corral busy with other broncs he'd look thru the bars for any show of interest in the little horse; he'd look often but most every time that pony's position was about the same, and if he did catch him with his head down he noticed how Smoky was just nibbling at the feed, and not eating much.

Smoky was taking the change, from the life he'd led to what he was now going thru, kinda hard, harder than the average wild horse ever does; and Clint layed it that the little horse had more brains than the average, more sensitive maybe, and more able to realize.

"I guess I'd better lay off of him to-day," decides the cowboy, as he noticed very little change in him even late that afternoon, "he's having a hard time trying to figger things out as it is."

It was bright and early the next morning when Clint looked out of the bunk house door and noticed Smoky out on the creek bottom. It appeared that the little horse, after figgering and figgering, had come to some sort of decision, and that done and settled had went to eating again, for that's what he was doing when Clint looked out,—Smoky was eating like he was trying to make up for the time he'd lost, and he seemed all at peace with everything in general.

The cowboy grinned, "I know what that son of a gun has decided on," he remarked. "He's going to fight, and I see where I'm sure due for a tossing from that pony to-day."

Clint done his day's work, and after riding and lining out nine head of rough and kinky broncs, went to where Smoky was picketed and led him into the corral where he'd been initiated a couple of days before. He was some kind of a different horse than what he'd been that day; his head was higher and more with just one purpose. He didn't shy and snort at every little thing like he did that first time, and Clint noticed that he never seemed to see the saddle as it was eased on his back and cinched.

"I don't like the sound of them 'rollers' that's making that noise in them nostrils of yours," he remarked; "they sound to me like you meant business."

Smoky did mean business, and even tho Clint was doing considerable kidding, he meant business too. He wasn't going to let the little horse get away with anything, for he realized that if he did it'd be harder than ever to persuade him to be good; he'd have to be treated rough, and Clint didn't want to treat him rough.

The cowboy seen the light in Smoky's eyes and understood it, he understood his every action, and they all meant fight.

"I'm glad to see so much spirit in you, old boy," he says as he pulled his hat down, "but if you want to fight I'll have to fight too, and here's hoping the best one of us wins;—let's go."

Smoky only shook his head a little as Clint put his hand on his left eye and mounted, he didn't want to notice a little thing like that, which was just as much a warning from him for that cowboy to get set, set well and solid, for in this next performance things was a going to pop worse than ever.

There's a big difference between the bucking that comes with the first setting of a bronc and the bucking that comes with the settings that follows afterwards on that same bronc. The first time Smoky was rode he was just a plain scared pony, of course his intentions was all to the good towards throwing that cowboy, saddle and all, off, but he was too scared and desperate to try and figger out how that should be done. He'd learned from that first setting that plain bucking wouldn't faze that rider, he'd have to use some science, and with a cool head, study out the weak points the rider might have, and work on them weak points till a shadow on the ground tells him the cowboy is *leaving*.

Smoky had learned that it wouldn't get him anything to stampede hot headed into bucking like he did that first time, maybe that's what he'd been studying on the last day or so. Anyway, he was some cool horse, and when he "bowed his head" this time it was all done deliberate and easy. He lined out with a few easy jumps just to sort of feel out how that cowboy was a setting as

81

a preliminary, and with an eye back on all the movements of the rider as he went, he layed his plans on just how to proceed and get his man.

It was just when Clint seemed to be riding his easiest when without warning Smoky "broke in two" and brought out some mighty wicked saddle-twisting, and cowboy-loosening jumps; crooked, high, and hard hitting was them jumps. It looked to the horse like his man was loosening at the sudden turning of events and had been shifted to one side a little,—and that's just what Smoky was looking for to carry on the program he'd mapped out.

It was the first encouragement that pony'd got since he first felt a rope on him, maybe he could get it over that cowboy yet. He bucked all the harder from the new energy the signs of winning brought him. No chance did he give so that the cowboy would ever get back in the saddle and straight up, and every jump from then on was used as a kind of leverage against the rider,—he bucked in a circle and every time he'd hit the ground he was his whole length back from where he'd started up.

The cowboy was well up on the fork of the saddle and still to one side. Smoky bucked on, and cool as a cucumber in a mountain stream, kept a watching and took care that he didn't buck back under him. He was holding his own, and looked for signs of the rider loosening some more, but no sign of that showed. The cowboy was still to one side and well up in the saddle, but he sure hung there, and with his left hand on the "Mecate" (hackamore rope) he kept his right up in the air and fanned on the same as ever.

As the fight kept on and no show of the cowboy ever loosening up any more was seen, Smoky begin to wonder. He'd tried different tactics and with all his figgering and variety of sidewinding he couldn't tear away from that hanging hunk of humanity. He was getting tired, his lungs begin to call for air and pretty soon he wasn't so cool no more.

All that was in him, science and everything, was brought out on a few more earth shaking jumps, and when a glance back showed Smoky the rider was still setting there, he got desperate again and begin to see red. He bellered and at the same time forgot all he'd studied on in the ways of getting his man.

The fight didn't last long after that, it was too furious and unscientific. Smoky fought the air, the earth, and everything in general,—nothing in particular was his aim, and pretty soon he lined out in long easy crowhops and then a standstill.

Clint climbed off as Smoky stood spraddle-legged and took in the air. The little horse never seemed to notice him and in a hazy way felt the rider's hand rubbing around his ears and straightening out his mane.

"I knowed you'd give me a tossing to-day," says Clint.

And there was one thing Smoky didn't know: it was that no time during the fight did the cowboy feel he was losing his saddle; a setting to one side the way he had been was just a long-staying holt of his, something like a half nelson with the wrastler.

Poor Smoky had lost again, but in a way he'd won,—he'd won the heart of a cowboy, cause, thru that fight that cowboy's feelings was for the little horse. He'd seen,

83

understood and admired the show of thinking qualities and the spirit which was Smoky's.

The idea might be got, on account of Smoky being the steady loser, that his spirit would get jarred and finally break, but if anybody thinking so could of seen that horse the next day that idea would of been scattered considerable. His time on the picket rope had been spent on *more* thinking and figgering, and the way he went after the tall grass showed he meant to be in shape to carry thru whatever the new scheme was.

And some would of thought it queer to've seen how Smoky, the steady loser in the contest, seemed to hold no grudge or hate against the winning cowboy. As it was, that pony seemed to welcome that human a lot as he walked towards him the next morning, and the way he rubbed his head against the shoulder of that smiling rider showed that the fights in the corral had got to be some friendly. Both was mighty serious, and both meant to win in them fights, but soon as they was over and the dust cleared there was a feeling the likes of when two friends have an argument; when the argument comes to an end both the loser and winner are ready to grin, shake hands, and be friends again.

Smoky had lost out twice in trying to dodge out from under his man, but he was nowheres near convinced as yet that it couldn't be done. The third time Clint climbed him that pony bucked harder than ever and that cowboy just sat up there and let him. Clint had whipped *some* horses for bucking that way, but he'd whipped them be-cause it was natural orneriness that made 'em buck. With Smoky it was different, there was no meanness in him so far,—that pony was confident that nothing could set him once he got onto the hang of knowing how to buck real well, and all he wanted was to be *showed* for sure that Clint could really set there and ride him thru his worst that way. After that was done he'd most likely quit.

The first couple of times Smoky was rode and after he'd quit his bucking, there hadn't been much more to it excepting that Clint would just run him around a bit and turn him a few times till the hump was well down on that pony's back. Smoky had got to thinking that was all would ever come of being corraled and saddled, and so, he was some surprised, when after the bucking spell was over at that third setting, to see the corral gate opened wide, the cowboy on him again, and heading him for open country.

Smoky took to the high ridges like a duck takes to water, he trotted out like a good horse, and then was put into a long lope. Covering territory felt mighty good to the little horse for a change and he wasn't caring much where the cowboy lined him out to. For a spell he'd forgot the weight on his back, his ears was straight ahead, and the hands he felt on his neck only reminded some that somebody was *with* him.

He was needing that change after being bested again like he'd been that third time. Clint had won once more and Smoky was a lot in favor of something, most anything, to drive off the feeling he'd got in losing. He was taking advantage of the run in that way and sashayed at a good clip. All went fine, till, of a sudden a jack rabbit scared out of his hiding place jumped up and

85

right under Smoky's nose,—he shied straight up and to one side, and at the same time he was scared more by the wing of Clint's chap which had curled up and slapped along his shoulder. Away he went to bucking once again.

The first few jumps was mighty wicked but they didn't last; he'd already had his buck out not long before and pretty soon he straightened into a lope once again. Clint let him lope a ways then turned him and headed him back to the corrals, stopped him there, turned him a few times and started him out a ways only to turn him and bring him back again. That went on for a few minutes, and then Smoky was unsaddled and put on the picket rope once more.

The run had tired Smoky a little and give him an appetite. He didn't do so much figgering on how to get his man that night, and instead he grazed more, rested some, and even slept a little. When he was led to the corral the next day and the saddle put on he even neglected to watch the cowboy and begin to show interest in the broncs that was in another corral. His ambitions hadn't allowed him to do that before, but somehow, things had changed.—Figgering ways and means of throwing off that rider had got to be tiresome, specially when nothing but disappointment was ever got by it; and besides that saddle and man was getting so they wasn't so bad to stand up under no more.

But as neutral as Smoky showed and felt, that little son of a gun bucked again. Of course there was nothing in his bucking that was so wicked as it had been in them first three saddlings; it was more that he felt he should buck *some*; it made him feel better, and besides he was wanting exercise; but he raised the dust and pounded the earth in good shape even at that, and that play of his would of throwed many a man.

Another run like the one of the day before, a few turnings and teachings on the feel of the rein, and Smoky was thru for another day. He was getting used to the lay of the program Clint had set, and the new game that was brought on right along as he was rode begin to draw the pony's interest.

Then one day, the cowboy begin dragging a rope on him; he let it drag quite a ways, and even tho Smoky watched it mighty close so it wouldn't circle around his legs and throw him like most ropes always did, it didn't worry him much. Pretty soon Clint coiled the rope up and made a loop which he started whirling in the air,— the whirling was slow and easy at first and done with a small loop. Smoky looked back all interest and snorted a little; he wondered what the rope was doing up there and what Clint was up to.

But nothing happened only that the whirling kept up, the loop was gradually made bigger and then it was throwed on the ground a ways in front of him. Smoky shied and snorted and the coils shot out, straightened, and all of it pulled up again by the cowboy; but he didn't try to run away from it, he hadn't forgot the eddication he'd received from the long soft picket rope. He'd learned from it that it didn't pay to stampede when a rope was around, on account that them ropes had a way of stopping him that couldn't at all be argued with.

Loops was made, throwed out, and drug in again one right after another. They went one side one time, and another side the next, then in front and back, till Smoky begin to lose fear no matter which way the rope went or how it coiled up. It was at the point when he was beginning to lose interest in the game that Clint roped a small bush. The rope tightened on it and Smoky pulled, —he pulled more in wonder what was holding him than with the idea of what he should do, but anyway the bush came out and headed straight for Smoky as it did, he struck at it and would of left from there, but Clint held him and made him face it.

Smoky shook like a leaf as slow but sure the cowboy kept a pulling the bush towards him, he struck again and snorted as it touched his front feet, and he bucked a couple of jumps when he felt it up along his shoulder, but there was no getting away from it; the way that bush moved, it looked like something vicious to Smoky, and when Clint took the rope off of it, and held it out under the pony's nose for him to see what it was the little horse near showed signs of shame for getting scared.

Loose stumps, branches, pieces of old wagons, and everything that could be drug or moved was roped,— anything that was light enough was pulled up for Smoky to investigate, and each time he was showed that he'd been shying and fighting for no reason, till finally, nothing could be found that brought any more than a snort from him. An old coal oil can was then roped and brought up a rattling under Smoky's nose, but he even stood his ground at that.

He was learned to pull on the rope and made to drag things as heavy as a yearling critter. Then gradually Clint made him keep the rope tight and hold it that way till a couple of light jerks on it made him give slack. All that took time, and the cowboy learned him only one thing each day, sometimes very little of that one thing, —but as the days went by it all accumulated to a lot.

It done Clint's heart good to watch the way Smoky was taking to things, his little ears worked back and forth, and with his eyes he never missed a move that went on; his nostrils quivered at all that was new, and the cowboy was noticing with a glad feeling that the pony was putting a lot of trust in him. A word from that cowboy, or a touch from his hand, was getting to mean a lot when that pony was dubious or at the point of scaring at some new happening.

Clint hunted up a bunch of cattle one day and acquainted Smoky with some pointers in the handling of the critters. He'd haze the horse in the bunch, cut out some fat kinky yearling, and make him put his interest on that yearling only. All was a puzzle to Smoky at first, and he had no idea of what he should do, but Clint give him his time, and coaching him along it wasn't but a few days when the little horse understood some of what was wanted of him. In the meantime the teachings with the rope wasn't left behind; that went along with working cattle, and once in a while Clint would snare some big calf and make Smoky keep his nose along that rope while the calf circled, bucked, and bellered.

Smoky showed signs of liking all that went on. He took interest in it the same as a kid would to some new game,—he liked to chase the wild eyed cow, turn her when she didn't want to be turned, and put her where she didn't want to be put; he liked to hold the rope tight on one of the critters and feel that *he* was the one that was keeping 'er down. It all struck him as a kind of a game where every animal before him had to do as *he* and the cowboy wished.

He was all for catching on and not a nerve in him was idle as Clint would take him of evenings and ride him out for a spell, and chase, cut out, or rope at the critter. Them goings on had his mind occupied and the fact that he'd figger and think on the subject between times was proved by the way he'd go at things in a decided and knowing how way, when the day before the same thing had left him puzzled and wondering.

That little work he was getting and the all heart interest he was finding in it, had settled him to the big change from the free life he'd led with the old buckskin horse and the bunch of mares and colts,—his mammy was even forgotten, and instead there'd sprouted in him something that made him take a liking for the long lanky cowboy that came to see and *play* with him every day. He'd got to finding a lot of pleasure in doing just what that cowboy wanted him to do, and when that was done there was a hankering in him to do just a little bit more.

That's the way Clint wanted to keep him; just a hankering to do more would get results, and he was careful to see that the little horse didn't tire on the work. He wanted to make it play for him and keep it that way as long as he could, for he knowed that was the way to keep Smoky's heart and spirit all in one hunk and intact.

6

CAN A HORSE KNOW TOO MUCH?

by GENEVIEVE TORREY EAMES

"NO, SIR, it's like I always said, it ain't good for a horse to know too much. A horse can be too smart—and that goes double for ponies. Ponies are generally smarter than horses to begin with."

John shook his grizzled head and wiped an imaginary speck of dirt from the little Welsh mare's glossy black neck. Ten-year-old Peter, standing beside the old man, flung a glance across the stable yard to the big stone house in the distance. He wanted to be sure that his father wasn't coming along to hear these doubts about the new pony. As for her, she tossed her head and laid back her ears.

"See that, now?" John went on. "She acts as if she heard what I said and felt unfriendly. I'm afraid Lightfoot is gonna make trouble."

Peter looked up anxiously at the man's face. "Oh, John, I think she's beautiful. And you said yourself it was time we turned Mousie over to Susan and got a bigger pony for me to ride. Don't you like her?"

"Never said I didn't like her," the old man grumbled. "Only I'm glad your Dad got her on trial, so we can see how she acts. She's a good-looking pony, all right, and she sure can jump. If she had plain pony brains, I dunno where you could find a better pony, now you've out-grown old Mousie." He stopped for a moment and kicked at the soft ground with the toe of his worn riding boot. "But that's just it," he went on more slowly. "She ain't got pony brains; she's got brains like a human, and that's not right. It's not—well, natural."

"What do you mean?"

"Well, the other day when she first came, I turned her out in the paddock to get a drink and she came right back into the barn. She unhooked the grain room door with her nose and walked in and started to help herself to the oats. And that ain't all. I know she's not the first horse ever to get a door open, and maybe she's had experience with that kind of hook before. That's smart, but not too smart. But wait, I'll show you. It's time to feed her, anyway."

He led Lightfoot back to her stall and tied her up. Peter followed, keeping at a respectful distance from the pony's heels.

John brought a forkful of hay and put it in the low manger in front of the pony. Peter sat, chin on hands, and kept his eyes on the pony. Lightfoot pulled at the hay, tossing her head restlessly. She soon had the hay on the floor and started to eat, pawing constantly with one forefoot as she did so.

"Why does she do that?" Peter asked.

"Dunno," John replied. "It's a habit. Lots of horses

paw while they eat. Seems to show they're enjoying their food."

"But look, John, she's pawed most of the hay so far back she can't reach it."

"Just you watch now, and you'll see what I'm talking about."

Lightfoot reached back as far as the halter rope would let her and nibbled at the few remaining wisps that she could reach. Then, as if by accident, she slid her right forefoot a few inches forward, bringing with it a small bunch of hay. When she had eaten that, she stepped back a little and again shuffled her feet forward until another mouthful of hay was within reach of her twitching nose.

"But, John," Peter asked in excitement, "does she do that on purpose?"

"She sure docs. I been watching her three evenings in a row. And just look at this now." He picked up the fork and put a morsel of hay over at one side of the stall. Lightfoot stretched out her neck, but the rope was too short.

"Oh, John," cried Peter. "You're teasing her. That's mean!"

John held his finger to his lips. "Wait," he whispered.

Lightfoot reached across with her left forefoot and dragged the tempting mouthful in front of her right hoof and then slid it along the floor to her nose, as before.

"Gee, she *is* smart," said Peter. "Smart as any horse in the circus, I betcha."

The old man shook his head. "Now that's what I say is against nature. A horse paws for excitement or be-

93

cause he feels good, and his legs just naturally paw from front to back. He can't help it. But when he starts pawing the other way, bringing back the hay he can't reach, and using two feet almost like a pair of hands, that's thinking, and not horse thinking either. It's *human* thinking!"

Peter sighed. "I just love her, John. Don't you think she'll be all right after she gets used to me? I mean, it would be just grand to have a pony as smart as that."

John hung up the fork and started for the rain room. "I dunno," he said. "You're a pretty good rider for your age and you can manage any ordinary pony that's not downright vicious. But this one, any time she starts to think up tricks, they won't be ordinary pony tricks. You don't know enough to outsmart a pony that don't think like a pony. Still, you be down here bright and early tomorrow and we'll see how she behaves."

He turned and looked sharply at the boy. "No oversleeping now. That's for city folks. If you can't get in your morning ride before school, guess we'll have to give it up—give up school, I mean."

But Peter did not ride the next morning. He was up extra early and ran to the stable to help John. "That's right," said John. "You give Lightfoot a drink while I finish cleaning the stalls."

Peter led the pony out to the paddock and turned her loose to drink. Highboy, the hunter, was dipping his muzzle in the clear, cold water in the concrete tank. Mousie had finished drinking and was rolling happily in the dust.

Lightfoot did not go near the water. Paying no attention to the other horses, she walked to the paddock

94

fence. Her head was high, ears forward, nostrils sniffing the sharp air. She seemed to be looking at the wooded hill across the road and she started pacing restlessly back and forth along the fence, keeping her head toward the hill as she walked. For a moment she stopped to scratch her neck against the top rail of the barway that led to the road. The rail loosened and one end clattered to the ground. In a flash Lightfoot jumped the lower bars and started for the road at a high trot. John came to the stable door just as Highboy and Mousie followed her lead, tails and heads high, hoofs flying.

"That pesky pony!" exclaimed John. "Making trouble already, just like I said. Here, Peter, take this rope and follow them. I'll get some oats."

The three horses crossed the road and dashed gaily up the grassy slope beyond. By the time John had joined Peter, Highboy and Mousie had settled down quietly to graze. Lightfoot, however, had not stopped for so much as a nibble of the rich grass. At a fast, steady trot she headed for the woods and disappeared in the fringe of young birches along the edge of the field.

John's face wore a puzzled look. "I can't figger that out," he said. "Can't see why she'd take to the woods and leave all this good feed. It ain't natural."

"Shall we follow her?" asked Peter anxiously.

John shook his head. "Got to get the other two in, first. Can't have them roaming all over the country. Chances are Lightfoot will come back when she finds the others haven't followed her. Horses usually stick together."

He gave a clear, long whistle and began shaking the oats in the measure he was carrying. Highboy and

Mousie raised their heads and trotted obediently across the grass to John. He gave them each a handful of oats, and Peter snapped the rope on Highboy's halter. John left Peter to watch for Lightfoot, while he led the hunter back to the stable, with Mousie following behind.

There was still no sign of Lightfoot when John came back. Inside the woods there was no chance of tracking the pony, and not a sound could be heard except the faint rustling of leaves in the treetops. Presently John gave up.

"Looks like the ground swallowed her," he said to Peter. "Anyway, she wouldn't go straight over the mountain unless something was chasing her. She'll most likely take it easy along the side of the hill and gradually work down into the open."

"What do we do now?" asked Peter.

"Guess you'll have to run along to school. I'll take Highboy, later, and go looking in the clearings along the base of the hill. Most likely I'll have her back by the time you get home."

But Lightfoot was still missing that afternoon, and John was grumbling about his wasted day. "That pony's more trouble than she's worth," he said. "If your Dad takes my advice, he'll take her right back where she came from. That is, if we ever do find her."

Peter could eat hardly any supper that evening. Nobody had a good word to say for Lightfoot, and he knew his father was annoyed and worried. His mother had telephoned an advertisement to the paper and had notified the police and the State Troopers. Yet no word had come in about a stray black pony.

The next day was Saturday. There was no school for

Peter, and his father stayed home from the office to help with the search.

"It's hard to know where to look," he said to John. "I can't imagine any horse going over that steep ridge if she didn't have to, and you say you've looked in all the likely places on this side."

"That's right, Mr. Davis," John answered. "There's hundreds of acres of woods along that ridge, but she wouldn't stay in the woods, and I've scoured the clearings and meadows all the way to Edgehill Station."

"You know what I think?" asked Peter suddenly. "I think she went straight over the mountain. She was headed that way and she was going fast. I don't think she'd stop for anything. She acted as if she had something on her mind."

The two men turned to look at Peter. "Could be you're right, at that," said John. "We've been trying to figger what an ordinary horse would do, and she's not ordinary. Yes, sir, I'll bet she had something on her mind—some deviltry no ordinary horse could think of."

Mr. Davis nodded. "Then the thing to do is to take the river road and start searching the farms on the other side. Whose place is directly opposite here? Jackson's, isn't it?"

The men jumped into the pick-up truck and took Peter on the seat between them. In a short time they were rolling along the river road on the far side of the ridge. John stopped the truck at a neat-looking farmhouse with the name Jackson on the mailbox.

A tall man in overalls was coming out of the barn. He grinned broadly when Mr. Davis mentioned the word pony. "A black pony, did you say? Yes, I guess I have

seen her, and I'll be glad to see the last of her." He led
the way around the barn to a pasture gate, and there
on the other side was Lightfoot, licking steadily at something that looked like a large white brick.

"Salt!" John exclaimed. "Acts like she's been salt-
starved for months."

"But our horses all have salt, don't they?" asked
Peter's father.

"Yes, I keep a block in each stall," John answered.
"But I hadn't any for Lightfoot when she came, and
when I ordered some, the feed company was all out.
Said they'd send some in a few days. I never thought
she'd be that crazy for it."

"How do you suppose she knew where to come for
the salt?" Mr. Davis asked.

John shook his head. "It beats me. I know a horse can
smell water quite a distance and I suppose he can smell
salt, but this is almost too far away. Looks like she just
wanted salt and set out to find it."

"I think that's smart of her," Peter broke in, and he
knew at once that it was the wrong thing to say.

"Smart, yes, too smart. That's what I've been saying
was the matter with this pony. A horse should depend
on his master and not start out on his own every time
he wants something."

"I don't know how she got into my pasture," Mr.
Jackson said. "She spent most of yesterday hanging
around that salt. That was all right with me, even when
she drove the cows away and wouldn't let them have
any. I knew somebody'd come looking for her sooner
or later.

"But after I took the cows in last night, the trouble

really began. She crashed the pasture gate, nosed around the pig pen until she let all the pigs out, got into the cow stable and upset a pail of milk, and then pushed the cover off the barrel of oats and helped herself. I was afraid to leave her in the pasture after that, and I haven't any extra stalls, so I had to put my work-team out in the pasture overnight and tie her up in the stable."

"Well," said Mr. Davis, "I'm glad we've found her. What do I owe you for all the damage?"

"Oh, nothing at all. Only I hope she doesn't get away again. She sure can get into a lot of mischief. I guess she'd wreck the place completely in three days."

They loaded Lightfoot into the truck and Peter rode in back with her on the way home. He could not hear what the men were saying, but he was sure they were talking about the pony. He was afraid they would decide to send her back, maybe today, before he'd even had a chance to ride her.

Unhappily, he pressed his face against the pony's heavy mane. "Oh, Lightfoot," he whispered. "Why can't you be good? If you just wouldn't make any more trouble, and if you'd only, *only* just like me a little bit, we could have neat fun together."

Lightfoot cocked her ears forward. Then she gave Peter a little nudge with her nose. "Oh," he sighed happily. "I believe you are beginning to like me, after all."

Mr. Davis looked thoughtful when they reached home. "Peter," he said, "I hate to disappoint you about Lightfoot, but it does look as if she's going to be too troublesome. So don't get your heart set on her. If she's going to be too independent, we'll have to send her back and

99

get another pony—one that thinks like a pony, as John says. But since she's here, you can try her out a few days longer."

In spite of John's doubts, the pony behaved well with her new rider, and for several days all went smoothly. John had nailed up the bar-way and fastened all the gates securely, and Lightfoot had no chance to escape.

Every morning Peter and John took a ride before breakfast. Peter loved the little mare and he was proud of her. He looked back on the days when he had ridden Mousie as if they had been ages ago. Mousie was all right for his little sister; she was only five. He saw nothing out of the way in Lightfoot's knowing more than most horses. It was what he expected of her.

Peter was learning to jump. When he and John took their morning rides they sometimes rode across the fields, jumping the stone walls and fences whenever they came to a low place. Peter was not quite sure of himself. It was fun and thrilling and just a little scary, too.

One morning they had started earlier than usual and were riding over strange country. It was near the end of the week and nothing more had been said about sending Lightfoot back. Peter was beginning to hope his father would decide to keep her.

There was a touch of frost in the air and the horses danced and fretted with eagerness. Peter's eyes were shining and his cheeks were red from the cold air. He was gaining confidence every day. "Race you across the field!" he cried, and was yards away before John could answer.

John touched his heels to the old hunter's sides and galloped easily after the pony. They slowed up as they

She inched slowly backward

came to the edge of the field. There was a low wall between them and a hilly pasture lot on the other side. The pony popped over and the hunter took it in his stride.

John pulled up a little. "That's enough," he called. "It's bad going here—got to take it easy." But Peter was away again, faster than ever. Maybe he hadn't heard, or perhaps, as was more likely, Lightfoot had decided things for herself.

John hesitated. His horse could overtake the pony easily on the flat, but the pony had the advantage on this rocky hillside. If it were a runaway, it would only make her run faster to hear the hunter galloping behind. He pulled Highboy to a slow trot and watched anxiously. It was too late now to catch up with them. He could only follow at a distance, hoping and praying.

Peter did not seem to be trying to stop, and Lightfoot ran as if she intended to go on for miles. They came to the edge of the pasture at last, where a low wall ran along the top of a steep bank. Below was an old lane, unused except for bringing cattle in from pasture. Lightfoot went over the wall and dropped out of sight in the lane.

John, riding faster now, caught sight of her a few seconds later as he reached the wall. He slid from the big horse and left him standing with reins dangling. He scrambled down the bank on the other side, his knees trembling and his voice shaking with fear. "You stay right there, Peter," he called. "Don't you move. I'll get you out. I'll get you out."

Some one had been pulling down the old barbed wire from the pasture fences and had left it—a great, wicked, jagged heap—in the lane, to be picked up and hauled away by a truck. Into the heap, which she could not see until it was too late to stop, Lightfoot had jumped. The long, snake-like coils wound around her legs and over her back. The barbs bit into her skin.

Peter, thoroughly frightened, clung to her mane. He would be in the midst of the wire if he got off. He was in just as much danger if he stayed on and the pony should begin to struggle.

John was at the edge of the wire, pulling at it with his bare hands, trying to loosen some of the strands so he could get near enough to lift Peter down.

"Don't you move, little pony," he said. "Don't you start threshing around—not yet. Just give us a chance here." His trembling fingers tore at the wire. Like something alive, it fastened its teeth in his clothes and held him.

Lightfoot looked at the old man with her wide-set, intelligent eyes. Then she turned her head and looked about her, on each side and behind her. Then she did a surprising thing. Slowly and carefully she picked up one foot, found it free of the wire, and put it down in a clear spot a few inches to the rear. One after another she moved each of her feet, inching slowly backward, pausing to see her way. Once she seemed to step deliberately on a strand of wire, holding it down while she moved her other foot.

John stopped wrestling with the wire and held his breath to watch. Then he called softly, "Put your head down against her neck, Peter." Peter obeyed and shut his eyes, clasping his arms about her neck.

At last the pony's hind legs were free, but still John

did not move. The wire was still snarled about her knees. There was a chance that she might start to jump and struggle, horse-fashion, and throw herself and Peter into its coils. But Lightfoot took another careful backward step and another, and they were clear.

Breathing a deep sigh of relief, John pulled his clothes loose from the wire and went around to Lightfoot's head. When he had led her out into the lane, well away from the wire, he looked Peter over carefully. A slight scratch on one hand was all he could find. Lightfoot had a few cuts about her legs but nothing serious.

Highboy had gone home but John did not mind. Peter would not ride while John walked, so together they led Lightfoot slowly back across the hills, talking as they went. The pony's ears twitched back and forth as if she understood what they were saying about her.

"I reckon," John was saying, "I reckon a horse can't know too much, after all. Any other horse I ever saw would have threshed around till she had herself, and you, too, all torn to bits. But this pony, she's different. She don't think like a pony, she thinks like a human."

"Sure thing," said Peter. "I knew it all the time." And he laughed aloud. For now he knew that Lightfoot was his for good.

7

SCOTT MAKES GOOD

by Col. S. P. Meek

"BOY, you sure got a break this time," chuckled Sergeant Winsoton as he entered the headquarters corral.

Sergeant Baker looked up, his tight lips parted in a smile.

"You mean about Snake-foot getting shanghaied to Corozal?" he asked.

"That and Scott coming down here. Think of it, Pete, a real he-man instead of that gentleman by act of Congress, a four-goal handicap Number Two and the best horseman in this man's army. Hi-lee, hi-lo," Winsoton chortled in glee and executed a few clumsy dance steps. "And he won't tell me to take any exercise in this heat either," he exulted.

"I'll be glad to see him," replied Baker non-committally. "Just now the thing that tickles me is that Glover's leaving. That's a real break for the ponies."

"And for you too, you old owl," said Winsoton. "He'd have had you busted and on stable police in another three months if he'd have stayed here. I expected to see him throw you in clink yesterday."

"Oh, that!" Baker snorted in disgust. "I told you he wouldn't dare try that. He came down here an hour after Frog threw him to see me about it. He said he was sorry he lost his temper and thanked me for holding him back. Then he offered me ten dollars to keep my mouth shut."

"What did you do?"

"I said, 'Don't worry, Lieutenant, I won't admit that any officer of the Nineteenth tried to pull off a stunt like that. As for the money, I think you'd better use it to buy liniment for some of the horses you've beaten up.'"

Winsoton whistled.

"Boy, you've got nerve, plenty of it. What did Snake-foot do?"

"I thought for a minute he was going to take a poke at me, but he didn't. He stuffed the money back in his pocket and walked away without a word."

"He'd have got even though, if he'd have stayed," said Winsoton. "Still, no need to worry now. Scott will change all that."

"Do you still think he can ride Frog and get away with it?" asked Baker.

"Think so? Boy, I'll bet a month's pay against a Panamanian dime that he'll have Frog eating out of his hand in a month."

"I hope so," said Baker reflectively. "It's Frog's last chance. No one here can handle him and the Old Man says he'll have him condemned and shot as an outlaw if he cripples another man. When does Scott get here?"

"On the *St. Mihiel* next Friday."

"Well, I'll send Frog up to his quarters as soon as he gets here and see what he can do with him. I still think that horse has the makings of a fine charger if the right man gets hold of him."

"The right man will get him when Scott takes him in charge," said Winsoton confidently. "Now I've got to go over and start my gang of loafers polishing up the gee-gee's hoofs. Snake-foot would never notice a thing like that, but Scott sees everything about a horse or a mule at one glance. You send Frog up to him and watch the way he does things to him."

"All right, Tubby, I'll do it. I sure hope he can handle him."

Lieutenant Scott looked up from his unpacking as he heard the sound of hoofs approaching his quarters. Two horses stopped before the hitching-rack and he went to the door in time to see a stable orderly tie to the rack a beautiful dark bay gelding with black points.

"Whose horse is that?" he called as he admired the clean lines and intelligent head of the animal.

"The stable sergeant sent him up for the lieutenant," answered the orderly with a salute. "He's the fastest horse we have, but he's a little mean."

"Tell the sergeant that I'm much obliged. I'll be down to see him soon."

"Yes, sir," replied the orderly as he mounted and trotted off toward the corral.

Scott forgot his unpacking in the face of a newly acquired mount. He hastily buckled on a pair of spurs and went out to inspect it. As he crossed the road with the peculiar swinging stride which is both the distinguishing mark and the proud acquisition of the cavalryman, he looked every inch a horseman. His compact, closely-knit figure was only of middle height, but there was not an ounce of surplus flesh on him. Thin drawn and fine cut, he looked as though he could bear the brunt of work that would wear most men out and come up smiling for more. He removed his campaign hat and passed a thin, sinewy hand over his close-cropped blond curls as he approached the horse.

"Good boy," he said as he rubbed Frog's nose, his keen blue eyes glittering as they took in the satiny coat and the dainty hoofs of his new mount. "You look as if you had real speed. I think we'll get along together fine."

He stepped to the horse's side to adjust the saddle. Frog made a lightning-like grab and the lieutenant leaped back out of danger with the left sleeve of his shirt torn off. Frog's heels lashed out viciously, but Scott stepped back out of kicking range and looked at him with admiration.

"Plenty of pep, haven't you, pony?" he said lightly. "I guess we'll have to watch you rather closely for a while."

He shortened the halter-shank, adjusted the saddle to his liking, mounted, and rode to the corral.

"I'm Lieutenant Scott," he said to Sergeant Baker as he dismounted. "Thanks for sending me up this horse. He seems to be a little skittish."

"Well, sir," said Baker cautiously, "he hasn't been handled just right recently, but I think he's a good horse."

"No doubt about that," agreed Scott. "Let me see his descriptive card, will you?"

Sergeant Baker turned into the corral office and Scott's attention was drawn by two hundred and forty pounds of soldier standing at rigid attention, a wide smile on his broad face. Scott gazed at him for a moment in doubt and then recognition came.

"Why, Winsoton!" he exclaimed as he extended his hand. "I'm glad to see you. What are you doing here?"

"I'm chief cargador of the Fifty-Third Pack Train, sir," said Winsoton as he gripped the lieutenant's hand. "I'm sure glad to see the lieutenant again, sir."

"The Fifty-Third, eh?" said Scott. "I'll come down tomorrow and look your outfit over. Got your mules all shined up?"

"Yes, sir; every gee-gee's hoofs are polished. We'll be ready for the lieutenant any time."

"That's good, but what's happened to you? You've put on a good deal of weight since I saw you last."

Winsoton's face crimsoned.

"Well, sir, you see," he stammered, "we have a pretty good mess sergeant. . . ."

"I knew that without your telling me," laughed Scott. "I think about the first thing I'll do here is to start you on a course of exercises to reduce your weight. . . ."

There was a strangled laugh from Baker as Winsoton's jaw fell. Scott joined merrily in the laughter, then turned to take the descriptive card which Baker extended to him. He studied it carefully.

The official name of the horse was *Godofredo*, which was probably accounted for by the fact that he had been foaled in Costa Rica nine years earlier. He had been purchased by the army and shipped to the Canal Zone six years before, and the characters given him by several officers who had essayed to ride him bore mute witness to the stormy life he had led. "Outlaw,"

111

"vicious," "unmanageable," were only a few of them, but Scott passed lightly over these and centered his attention on one entry. One officer had given Frog a character of "excellent."

"Someone knew how to handle him and that proves he can be handled," he mused. "He has good gaits and is apparently sound. I'll make a good horse out of him yet."

"Why do you call him Frog?" he asked the stable sergeant.

"Well, sir, it's this way. Godofredo is too long for every-day use, so we gave him a nickname. We called him Frog because he has a habit of squatting down on his haunches and jumping just like a frog."

"Is he really vicious?"

"Yes, sir. Grooming him is a punishment detail. No one goes around his stall without carrying a pitchfork."

"No wonder the poor brute is vicious. That's no way to handle a horse. Have you an empty box stall?"

"Yes, sir."

"Take his harness off and turn him loose in it. Give orders that no one is to feed, water, or groom him, except myself."

Frog enjoyed the freedom of a box stall, but he had a reputation for viciousness to maintain and it took three dry days in the sultry heat of Panama to make him sufficiently thirsty to allow Scott to pick up and examine his hoofs without protest. It was another week before he would allow himself to be groomed without being tied, but Scott was blessed with the patience of Job and a deep sympathetic understanding of horse nature, and he did not try to rush matters. Frog gradually learned that the lieutenant was not intentionally hurting him, and finally tolerated him in his stall without protest. Scott made progress gradually, and in three weeks he was able to saddle and bridle Frog without first hitching him. At this point he determined to try him on the field.

He harnessed him with a light polo-saddle and a snaffle-bit, then led him out and mounted him. Toward the riding-field they went, Frog trotting along quietly with a gait that was a delight to his rider. The horse enjoyed the light saddle, and above all he liked the absence of the punishing curb to which he was accustomed.

Once on the riding-field, Scott slipped his feet out of the stirrups and put Frog through his paces and over the hurdles with no difficulty. Frog was wise in the ways of riders; and he knew that the man on his back had a firm seat, and that any attempt to unseat him would be futile until he was lulled into a sense of false security by the docile actions of his mount. He obeyed the orders given him by the lieutenant's spurs and reins, and bided his time.

Lieutenant Lacey rode past Scott and called to him. Scott reined in Frog and turned on his saddle to speak to the adjutant. This was the chance for which Frog had been waiting, and he stealthily crouched lower and lower. Like a spring his muscles contracted and then, like a spring uncoiling, he leaped straight forward, covering fifteen feet in one mighty bound.

This was the trick which had won him his nickname, and it had usually unseated his rider. But Frog had not reckoned with the skill of the man astride him. Scott slid back to the horse's croup, but he held his balance and scrambled back into the saddle as Frog hit the ground

113

and gathered himself for a buck. A dozen vicious bucks and a sunfish failed to rid him of his rider, and then a quirt bit into Frog's flank. He reared up and went over backwards, but his rider jumped clear. As Frog scrambled to his feet, Scott vaulted upon his back and drove his spurs deep into the horse's flanks.

Frog kicked violently, and turned his head, trying to seize Scott's knee in his teeth, but the punishing quirt smote him on the nose. With a scream of rage he grasped the bit in his teeth and bolted. Twice he tore around the field at full speed, and then the quirt fell on his flank again. Frog stopped with a sudden jar and reared to throw himself over backwards again. This time the loaded end of the quirt hit him between the ears and he went forward, groggy. He tried to grab the bit in his teeth again, but there was an iron hand on the reins and he could not reach it. Once more he essayed to buck, but the spurs struck home and he stopped, trembling, and waited for what might come.

As soon as Frog stood, Scott vaulted lightly from his back and approached his head. Frog laid his ears flat and bared his teeth, but the lieutenant laughed softly, grasped his lower jaw, and drew his head down.

"Steady, boy!" he said sternly. "What are you raising such a rumpus about? Behave yourself now."

The voice was friendly, and although Frog quivered a little as Scott's hand sought his nose, he stood waiting for his punishment. To his surprise, no punishment came. Instead of striking him, Scott stroked his nose gently, rubbed his ears, and then deliberately turned his back on him and walked off.

Frog could not understand such treatment. Always

114

before, one of his outbursts had been the signal for the arrival of men armed with pitchforks, who had beaten him severely. Here was a man who had not only been able to keep his seat against the worst that Frog could do, but also one who harbored no resentment against him. When the lieutenant remounted and rode him slowly around the field until he was dry, then took him to the corral, curried him carefully, and gave him a lump of sugar, Frog realized that Lieutenant Scott was different from the men who had tried vainly to master him.

"I rather expect that will be the end of the fireworks," Scott said to the admiring Lacey as they walked out of the corral together. "Tomorrow I'll take a stick and start making a polo pony out of him."

But Scott had reckoned without full knowledge of Frog's nature. For years the horse had been master of the men who had ridden him, and he did not mean to give up that supremacy without an effort. He might let Scott ride him for the exercise he got out of it, but he wanted it clearly understood that he was merely allowing himself to be ridden, and that the ride would end when Frog wished it to and not when the rider decided it would.

Scott was wise in the ways of horses, especially bad horses, and during the next two months Frog failed to unseat him. He taught the horse a great deal about polo, but at the end of that time he felt that he would never dare use him in a game where his attention would have to be on the ball and not on the horse, for every relaxation of the eternal vigilance he kept over his mount had resulted in a battle royal between them.

"I'm afraid that I'm beaten by a horse for once," he

confided to Captain Kildare, captain of the Nineteenth's polo squad. "I can ride Frog all right, if I keep my attention on him, but all the time I know that he's just waiting for a chance to police me."

"He's plain mean," replied Kildare. "I tried him out and gave him up a year ago, and Glover's manhandling of him since didn't improve his temper any. I don't think that anyone will ever win his affection or make him dependable."

"I'll try him for another month and then, if he keeps the same attitude, I'll turn him back and let someone else tackle him. He's the fastest and sturdiest horse we have, and he can turn around on a dime and hand you back a nickel change, but I know when I'm licked."

Scott rode Frog daily, striving by kindness, firmness, and every trick known to horsemanship to win him over, but he was forced to confess at the end of the time he had allowed himself that he did not dare relax his vigilance for a moment while he was mounted. He turned the horse back to Sergeant Baker and made a report to Colonel Bennitt. Since no other officer of the Nineteenth cared to try the task at which Scott had failed, Frog was duly listed as incorrigible and waited only for the next visit of the inspector to be condemned and shot.

The inspector came and started on his duties. Frog's doom was to be settled the next day. Scott paid the horse a visit, and his conscience smote him as he looked at the beautiful lines and intelligent head of the animal. He saddled him and rode him again, but at the end of an hour turned him back, announcing that, as far as he was concerned, the case was hopeless.

A dance in honor of the visitor was at its height in

the Officer's Club when the dull boom of the saluting-gun stopped the music and brought the officers to their feet, wondering as to the cause of the alarm. Their wonder was of short duration, for from the guard house and barracks the notes of fire-call sounded on the night air. Lieutenant Lacey rushed in from the telephone.

"The stables, gentlemen!" he cried. "Troop commanders will bring their organizations down on the double; junior officers will report to the scene of the fire."

Scott was the first of the officers to arrive at the burning stables and he sought out Sergeant Baker.

"Are all the horses out?" he asked.

"All out, sir, except three that are in the far corner of headquarters stable. No one can face that furnace."

The dry season was at its height in the Canal Zone. For four long, weary months no rain had given relief to the parched savannas. The cattle were dying of starvation on the ranges, and even the jungle swamps had dried out until the pack-trains could travel over the trails without encountering fetlock-deep mud. The grass and brush were dead and the buildings were as dry as a bleached bone. As Scott looked at the tinder-dry building which had flared up like oil-soaked paper, he realized the truth of Baker's statement. The headquarters stable was a seething mass of flames, and it seemed certain that no one could enter that roaring furnace and hope to live. The collapse of the roof was only a matter of moments and Scott marvelled that it had not already fallen.

As he stood there helpless, awaiting the arrival of the cavalry fire engines, the despairing scream of a trapped horse in an agony of fear struck his ears. Scott loved horses, and that wail of despair seemed to make an icy hand clutch at his heart and to chill the very marrow in his bones. He shuddered, and plugged his ears with his fingers, but the scream came again. With a start, Scott recognized the horse's voice.

"Frog!" he muttered.

He hesitated for a moment and then, as the scream rose a third time on the night air, he ran to the watering trough and leaped in. In a moment he was soaked to the skin. Dripping with water, he climbed from the trough and rushed headlong toward the burning building.

Frog had been awakened, with the other horses, by the acrid smell of smoke and the sight of flames flickering around the roof of the building. The tumult they had promptly raised had awakened the stablemen and resulted in the turning in of the alarm. Bravely the stable orderlies had gone into the burning building, and horse after horse had been blindfolded and led out to safety. But the flames had gained headway rapidly, and Sergeant Baker reluctantly ordered his men to cease their efforts and leave the last three horses to their fate.

Frog had vainly tried to kick out the door of his box stall, but it was too heavy for him to break. He strove to leap into the next stall, but there was no room for a take-off, and his efforts to climb out had been a failure. He raised his voice and cried out his fear, but no one heard or heeded. Aimlessly he charged about the narrow confines of the stall, kicking and crying out.

Suddenly the door flew open and a white-clad figure leaped into the stall, tearing off his coat as he did so. Frenzied with fear, Frog charged his rescuer, but he was met with a blow of a fist on the nose and a calm voice spoke.

"Steady, boy, steady!" it said.

The voice was familiar and Frog paused for an instant. In another moment the wet coat was over his head, shutting out the fearful sight of the flames and a well-known hand was on his mane, guiding him to safety.

A cheer broke from the watching soldiers as Scott led the horse from the doomed building, and none too soon, for a crash behind him told of the falling roof which shut off any further chance for rescues.

"Scott," cried Lacey, rushing up to him, "the telephone lines are down. Mount and ride all you know to Camp Gaillard and order their engine out. The storehouse will go in a few minutes if we don't get help."

Scott saluted, tore the coat from Frog's head and leaped upon him barebacked. Frog snorted and hesitated for a moment as the flames became visible, but the rider was familiar, and his voice was soothing. Besides, he ordered Frog to do just what he wished to do—leave that neighborhood in a hurry. Out of the corral like an arrow he flashed, his rider leaning forward over his neck and begging him for more speed. On through the night he thundered through Golden Green and up the Culebra Hill. As they reached the Camp Gaillard fire house, Scott placed his hands on Frog's neck and vaulted safely to the ground. Frog checked his gait, stopped and waited while the lieutenant hastily gave the orders which turned out the already-hitched fire engine and started it at a gallop toward Empire.

119

The two heavy fire horses drew the engine rapidly, but past them like a streak, flew Scott and Frog. On down the road and into the corral they raced, carrying the welcome word that help was at hand.

"Mr. Scott," cried Colonel Bennitt, "ride back to meet them and lead them over to the warehouse; tell them to turn their streams on the roof and try to keep the flames from spreading."

The shortest route led close by the remains of the headquarters stable, and without thought, Scott directed Frog toward it.

Frog hesitated for a moment and then, at an encouraging word from Scott, he charged forward, leaped over a burning timber, and passed the smoldering heap so close that Scott's white trousers were scorched. The oncoming engine was intercepted and directed to its position, and Scott returned to his former station to receive further orders. Another rafter had fallen and Frog had two burning barriers to face. He leaped each without hesitation and came to a stop before the colonel and the inspector.

"Where did you get that horse, Mr. Scott?" asked the inspector, a few moments later.

"He's a government horse, sir, one of my polo string. I mean he was one of my polo string. He is up before you for condemnation tomorrow for viciousness."

"If you can ride him around barebacked like that, he can't be so very vicious," remarked the inspector.

"I'll show you, sir," replied Scott. He deliberately raised his right leg and sat sideways on the horse, entirely helpless against a buck. This was the chance for which Frog had been waiting for three months. He stealthily gathered his muscles for a buck.

"Steady, boy," said a quiet voice in his ear and a soothing hand caressed his neck.

Gradually the horse relaxed his muscles and his ears perked upright. His drawn-back lips relaxed to cover his teeth and Frog turned his head and rubbed his nose gently against the lieutenant's knee.

"See, sir?" cried Scott in triumph, as he stroked the outstretched nose. "He's as gentle as a baby."

"So I see," replied the inspector. "I think he's safe to-morrow. He's not only gentle, he's also the nerviest pony I have ever seen."

"Wait until you see us on the polo-field, sir," said Scott happily, as he stroked Frog's neck. "This horse has brains as well as nerve. We'll show you some real polo when we get going!"

A few yards behind Scott and the inspector, two enlisted men had been deeply interested spectators of the scene. As Frog relaxed his muscles and turned to nuzzle his master, Sergeant Winsoton gave vent to a series of sounds meant to express extreme joy.

"I told you so, you old owl, I told you so!" he cried joyfully as he pounded Sergeant Baker on the back. "He's got Frog eating out of his hand right now. Boy, you owe me a good dinner at the American House next payday."

"It looks like it," answered Baker thoughfully. "If Frog still behaves by payday, I'll pay for that dinner more cheerfully than I've paid for anything for a year. But where do you get that gloat? Didn't I always say that Frog would make a wonderful polo pony if the right man ever got hold of him?"

"Aw, horsefeathers," chuckled Winsoton as he hugged himself and executed a few clumsy dance steps. "I'll take fried chicken—a double order."

°8°

THE BLACK STALLION
AND
THE RED MARE

by GLADYS F. LEWIS

AT FIRST Donald lay still. Scarcely a muscle moved. The boulders and the low shrubs screened him from view. Excitement held him motionless. His hands gripped the short grass and his toes dug into the dry earth. Cautiously he raised himself on his elbows and gazed at the scene below him.

There, in his father's unfenced hay flats, was the outlaw band of wild horses. They were grazing quietly on the rich grass. Some drank from the small hillside stream. Donald tried to count them, but they suddenly began moving about and he could not get beyond twenty. He thought there might be two hundred.

Donald knew a good deal about that band of horses, but he had never had the good luck to see them. They were known over many hundreds of square miles. They had roamed at will over the grain fields and they had

123

led away many a domestic horse to the wild life. Once in that band, a horse was lost to the farm.

There in the flats was the great black stallion, the hero or the villain of a hundred tales. Over the far-flung prairie and grass lands there was scarcely a boy who had not dreamed of wild rides, with the great body of the stallion beneath him, bearing him clean through the air with the sharp speed of lightning.

There was the stallion now, moving among the horses with the sureness and ease of a master. As he moved about, teasingly kicking here and nipping there, a restlessness, as of a danger sensed, stirred through the band. The stallion cut to the outside of the group. At a full gallop he snaked around the wide circle, roughly bunching the mares and colts into the smaller circle of an invisible corral.

He was a magnificant creature, huge and proudly built. Donald saw the gloss of the black coat and the great curving muscles of the strong legs, the massive hoofs, the powerful arch of the neck, the proud crest of the head. Donald imagined he could see the flash of black, intelligent eyes. Surely a nobler creature never roamed the plains!

Off-wind from the herd, a red mare came out from the fold of the low hills opposite. She stood motionless a moment, her graceful head held high. Then she nickered. The black stallion drew up short in his herding, nickered eagerly, then bolted off in the direction of the mare. She stood waiting until he had almost reached her; then they galloped back to the herd together.

The shadows crept across the hay flats and the evening stillness settled down. A bird sang sleepily on one note. Donald suddenly became aware of the monotonous song, and stirred from his intent watching. He must tell his father and help send news around the countryside. He was still intensely excited as he crept back from the brow of the hill and hurried home. All the time his mind was busy and his heart was bursting.

Donald knew that three hundred years ago the Spaniards had brought horses to Mexico. Descendants of these horses had wandered into the Great Plains. These horses he now was watching were of that Spanish strain. Thousands of them roamed the cattle lands north to the American boundary. This band now grazed wild over these park lands here in Canada—four hundred and fifty miles north of the boundary.

His father and the farmers for many miles around had determined to round up the horses and make an end of the roving band. As a farmer's son, Donald knew that this was necessary and right. But a certain respect for the band and the fierce loyalty that he felt toward all wild, free creatures made him wish in his heart that they might never be caught, never be broken and tamed. He, who was so full of sympathy for the horses, must be traitor to them!

There had been conflicts in his heart before, but never had there been such a warring of two strong loyalties. He saw himself for the first time as a person of importance because he, Donald Turner, had the power to affect the lives of others. This power, because it could help or harm others, he knew he must use wisely.

When he stood before his father half an hour later, he did not blurt out his news. It was too important for that. But his voice and his eyes were tense with excitement. "That band of wild horses is in the hay hollow, west of the homestead quarter," he said. "There must be close to two hundred."

His father was aware of the boy's deep excitement. At Donald's first words he stopped his milking, his hands resting on the rim of the pail as he looked up.

"Good lad, Donald!" he said, quietly enough. "Get your supper and we'll ride to Smith's and Duncan's to start the word around. Tell Mother to pack lunches for tomorrow. We'll start at sunup." He turned to his milking again.

The other men were in the yard shortly after daylight.

Donald afterward wondered how long it would have taken ranch hands to round up the band of horses. These farmers knew horses, but not how to round up large numbers of them as the men of the ranch country knew so well. The farmers learned a good deal in the next two weeks.

Twenty men started out after the band as it thundered out of the hay flats, through the hills and over the country. The dust rose in clouds as their pounding hoofs dug the dry earth. The herd sped before the pursuers with the effortless speed of the wind. The black stallion led or drove his band, and kept them well together. That first day only the young colts were taken.

At sunset the riders unsaddled and staked their horses by a poplar thicket, ate their stale lunches and lay down to sleep under the stars. Their horses cropped the short grass and drank from the stream. Some slept standing; others lay down.

At dawn the herd was spied moving westward. With the coming of night, they, too, had rested. For a mile or more they now sped along the rim of a knoll, swift as bronchos pulled in off the range after a winter out. The black stallion was a hundred feet ahead, running with a tireless, easy swing, his mane and tail streaming and his body stretched level as it cut through the morning mists. Close at his side, but half a length behind him, ran the red mare. The band streamed after.

After the first day's chase and the night under the stars, Donald had ridden back home. Not that he had wanted to go back. He would have given everything that he owned to have gone on with the men. But there were horses and cattle and chores to attend to at home, and there was school.

The roundup continued. Each day saw the capture of more and more horses. As the men doubled back on their course, they began to see that the wild horses traveled in a great circle, coming back again and again over the same ground, stopping at the same watering holes and feeding in the same rich grass flats. Once this course became clear, fresh riders and mounts in relays were posted along the way, while others drove on from behind. The wild band had still to press on with little chance for rest and feeding. The strain of the pursuit took away their desire for food, but they had a burning thirst and the black stallion would never let them drink their fill before he drove them on. Fatigue grew on them.

As the roundup continued, the whole countryside stirred with excitement. At every town where there was a grain elevator along the railroad, people repeated the latest news of the chase. On the farms the hay went unmown or unraked, and the plows rested still in the last furrow of the summer fallow. At school the children played roundup at recess. Donald, at his desk, saw the printed pages of his books, but his mind was miles away, running with the now almost exhausted wild horses.

Near the end of the second week of the chase, Donald's father rode into the yard. Donald dropped the wood he was carrying to the house and ran to meet his father.

"Dad, they haven't got the black stallion and the red mare, have they?" Donald could scarcely wait for his father's slow reply.

"No, Donald, lad," he said. "Though those two are the only horses still free. They're back in the flats. We'll get them tomorrow."

Donald felt both relief and fear.

In the yellow lamplight of the supper table his father told of the long days of riding, of the farms where he had eaten and rested, and of the adventures of each day.

"That was a gallant band, lad!" he said. "Never shall we see their equal! Those two that are left are a pair of great horses. Most wild horses show a weakening in the strain and grow up with little wind or muscle. But these two are sound of wind and their muscles are like steel. Besides that, they have intelligence. They would have been taken long ago but for that."

No one spoke. Donald felt that his father was on his side, the side of the horses. After a long pause, Mr. Turner continued.

"With his brains and his strength, that stallion could have got away in the very beginning. He could have got away a dozen times and would now be free south of the border. But that was his band. He stayed by them, and he tried to get them to safety. This week, when his band had been rounded up, he stuck by that red mare. She is swift but she can't match his speed. It's curious the way they keep together! He stops and nickers. She nickers in reply and comes close to him, her nose touching his flank. They stand a moment. Then they are away again, she running beside him but not quite neck to neck. Day after day it is the same. They are no ordinary horseflesh, those two, lad!"

There was a lump in Donald's throat. He knew what his father meant. Those horses seemed to stand for something bigger and greater than himself. There were other things that made him feel the same—the first full-throated song of the meadow lark in the spring; ripe golden fields of wheat with the breeze rippling it in waves; the sun setting over the rim of the world in a blaze of rose and gold; the sun rising again in the quiet east; the smile in the blue depths of his mother's eyes; the still whiteness of the snow-bound plains; the story of Columbus dauntlessly sailing off into unknown seas.

These things were part of a hidden, exciting world. The boy belonged to these things in some strange way. He caught only glimpses of that hidden world, but those glimpses were tantalizing. Something deep within him leaped up in joy.

That night Donald dreamed of horses nickering to him but, when he tried to find them, they were no longer there. Then he dreamed that he was riding the great, black stallion, riding over a far-flung range, riding along a hilltop road with the world spread below him on every side. He felt the powerful body of the horse beneath him. He felt the smooth curves of the mighty muscles. Horse and rider seemed as one.

129

A cold dawn shattered his glorious dream ride. With his father he joined the other horsemen. From the crest of the slope from which Donald had first seen them, the pair of horses was sighted. They were dark moving shadows in the gray mists of the morning.

They had just finished drinking deep from the stream. Not for two weeks had the men seen the horses drink like that. Thirsty as they were, they had taken but one drink at each water hole. This last morning they were jaded and spent; they had thrown caution to the winds.

At the first suspicion of close danger, they stood still, heads and tails erect. Then they dashed toward the protecting hills. There the way forked.

It was then Donald saw happen the strange thing his father had described. At the fork the stallion halted and nickered. The mare answered and came close. She touched his flank with her head. Then they bounded off and disappeared in the path that led northwest to the rougher country where the chase had not led before.

Along the way the horses had been expected to take, grain-fed horses had been stationed. These had now to move over northwest. But the men were in no hurry today. They were sure of the take before nightfall. The sun was low in the west when two riders spurred their mounts for the close in. The stallion and the mare were not a hundred yards ahead. They were dead spent. Their glossy coats were flecked with dark foam. Fatigue showed in every line of their bodies. Their gallant spirits no longer could drive their spent bodies. The stallion called to the mare. He heard her answer behind him. He slowed down, turning wildly in every direction. She came up to him, her head drooped on his flank

The stallion drew strength for a last mighty effort

and rested there. In a last wild defiance, the stallion tossed his magnificent head and drew strength for a last mighty effort. Too late!

The smooth coils of a rope tightened around his feet. He was down, down and helpless. He saw the mare fall as the rope slipped over her body and drew tight around her legs. It maddened him. He struggled wildly to be free. The taut rope held. The stallion was conquered. In that last struggle something went out of him. Broken was his body and broken was his spirit. Never again would he roam the plains, proud and free, the monarch of his herd.

Donald saw it all. He felt it all. His hands gripped the pommel of the saddle and his knees pressed hard against his pony's side. Tears blinded his eyes and from his throat came the sound of a single sob. It was as if he himself were being broken and tied.

The sun dipped below the rim of the plains. The day was gone; the chase was ended. The men stood about smoking and talking in groups of two's and three's, examining the two roped horses. Donald's father knelt close to the mare, watching her intently. Donald watched him. His father remained quiet for a moment, one knee still resting on the ground, in his hand his unsmoked pipe. Donald waited for his father to speak. At last the words came.

"Boys," he said, without looking up, and with measured words, "do you know, this mare is blind—stone blind!"

A week later, Donald and his father stood watching those two horses in the Turner corral. They were not

133

the same spirited creatures, but they were still magnificent horses.

"I figured," his father said, turning to the boy, "that they had won the right to stay together. I've brought them home for you, Donald. They are yours, lad. I know you will be good to them."

9

HIGH COURAGE

by C. W. ANDERSON

HOLLEY paused and looked for a long moment when a groom stripped the sheet from the black horse, Thunderer. He shook his head as he turned away. "I wish that horse wasn't here," he said.

"Yes, he's the one to beat," said Jack, his eyes following the sleek, powerful quarters. "He's fast."

Holley sighed, and turned to saddle Bobcat. The big horse moved and quivered and his eyes glowed with excitement. He snorted and stamped, all afire to be off, as Holley tightened the girth.

"Easy, now, easy," spoke Holley. "You'll be in it soon enough. You'll be in it right up to your neck, today. Better save all of that for later." Bobcat stamped and blew through distended nostrils as his eager head turned to follow everything that moved around him. "He feels mighty good, Mister Jack."

"No carrots today, eh, Holley?" The boy smiled; but his face felt stiff, as if the skin were drawn too tight.

Holley grinned. "He's a big boy now. No kid stuff for him today. He ain't going to refuse anything that's between here and there—not today." He slapped Bobcat's

135

shoulder. "All he needs is a horse to give him a fight—an' it looks like he gets it this time."

"Where's Miss Patsy, Holley? I thought she'd be in the paddock to see him saddled."

"She's too nervous an' wrought up, mostly worrying about something happening to Bobcat. She's up the slope a little way where she can see the race."

"There's a big crowd here," said Jack, looking over the gently sloping hill which served as a perfect grandstand.

It looked like a carpet of variegated colors. The grays and browns of tweeds and the brighter colors of sports clothes were broken by occasional patches of green. It seemed as if all Maryland had turned out for the race. Dotted at intervals over the green of the course were groups and clusters of spectators at almost every fence—people who preferred a close-up of the straining horses taking a jump to a complete but distant view of the course.

Patsy stood by herself; she did not feel up to talking to friends until the tension of the race had passed. Holley was coming back to see the race with her. For the crowds there was the spectacle of ten of the country's best jumpers competing for a historic cup; for Holley and herself there would be but one horse for their eyes to follow, with tense and breathless concern.

It was nearing post time and she caught scraps and tag ends of conversation and excited comment. "The black's the one—hasn't been beaten this year." "This new horse, Bobcat—ran a good race in the Harkaway Cup." "Only one race. Used to be a sulker—this course is no place for that sort." Then a man saying, "It's the third and thirteenth that puts them down. Five feet and solid as iron."

A bugle blew "Boots and Saddles" and the horses began to file out of the paddock. Most of them walked like old and tried campaigners, with here and there one fighting the bit in eagerness to be away. Now she could see Bobcat; he was prancing sideways, his head high, all fire and spirit. Jack, in his racing silks, looked slight and frail on the big horse. Thunderer was sent for a warm-up gallop and Patsy's heart sank when she saw his long, raking stride.

The horses were being lined up at the start when Holley arrived, breathless. "Hard to get through this big crowd," he said. "Bobcat's feeling good—never saw him so raring to go. Folks are going to see a real jumper today."

"But what about Thunderer, Holley? How can any horse beat him?"

"Yeah, he looks like quite a horse. Still, he ain't ever been over as long or tough a course as this. May not look so good if a horse gets to him near the end. They'll be off in a second, now!"

The starter's flag dropped and an excited cheer burst from the crowd as the field surged forward and raced for the first fence. Thunderer, already in front, took the fence in his stride; the rest of the field jumped almost together. As they landed, a chestnut pulled out of the line and moved powerfully a length behind the leader.

"Nice work, boy; nice jumping," said Holley.

Patsy held her breath as she watched them race for the next fence. Thunderer was outrunning Bobcat; he was two lengths in front as he rose to the second jump,

137

but as Bobcat put in a magnificent jump and strode on he was again only a length behind.

"He's gaining over the jumps an' that horse ain't running away from him," cried Holley exultantly. "We're going to do all right, Honey."

Now they were coming to the third fence, the biggest on the course. Thunderer and Bobcat were going at a terrific pace; the rest of the field was already well strung out behind them. The black had again increased his lead, and jumped the fence well in front. Bobcat rose to the fence in a tremendous arc, and a cheer followed the big horse as it was seen that he had gained two lengths and was lapped on the black to the girth.

"Man, man, but he's flying his fences today!" exclaimed Holley, and a warm feeling of pride and admiration drove some of the apprehension from Patsy's mind.

Two horses had fallen and another pecked badly and galloped off the course, riderless. The rest were over, but it seemed clear that the race was between the two horses in front if they kept their feet. At the fourth fence Thunderer led by an open length and again Bobcat closed most of the gap over the jump. They swung around the turn, and horses and men were seen in brilliant miniature across a half mile of undulating green. Despite the fast pace both horses seemed to be running easily. All the way around the first time they held the same positions with not more than a couple of lengths between them. Although the black seemed faster, Bobcat was clearly the bolder jumper. The third horse was ten lengths back, with the rest strung out.

Now they were coming to the twelfth fence, almost opposite the spot where Patsy and Holley stood. Again the big chestnut drew up on his rival as he swept over the fence in his stride and raced for the big thirteenth, that had proved unlucky to so many fine horses. It was a continuation of the third, flagged several panels farther away, and was five forbidding feet of heavy chestnut post and rail. Patsy, remembering how huge and solid it had looked when she stood beside it that morning, gasped when she saw the speed at which the two horses went at it.

"They're going too fast; they'll never make it!" she cried. Her nails dug into her clenched hands as she looked on helplessly.

Thunderer was over, although he rapped the top rail, and her heart seemed to stop as Bobcat jumped—then to race on as she saw that he had cleared it flawlessly. Again cheers greeted the magnificent performance.

"He's going grand, Honey," cried Holley joyfully, "an' he's got plenty up his sleeve." The horses had now swung around the turn. "A couple of more fences an' you'll see Mister Jack make his move. An' he's got an armful of horse."

Even as Holley spoke, Thunderer let out a notch and in a moment had opened up a four-length lead. The black horse flew at the eighteenth fence, hit the top rail hard, and barely escaped going down. The rider shot up on his neck and before they got into stride again Bobcat was leading by five lengths. Thunderer failed to cut down the lead appreciably as they reached the nineteenth, for now Bobcat had also let out a link and was running powerfully.

Both horses were going at racing speed down the slope to the twentieth.

"He's going awful fast," muttered Holley. "That's a mean fence, though it looks so small."

Patsy could see that Jack was trying to pull the big horse down, but without effect. They came into the fence too far away, hit it hard, and went down. Patsy gave a little gasp and a groan as Thunderer sailed over. Then she saw that Bobcat had plowed along on his knees and managed, by a tremendous effort, to stay up. Jack had gone over his head but was up in an instant and vaulted into the saddle and they were off in pursuit of the black, who now led by twenty lengths.

Down on the course Jack was desperately trying to find his stirrups before they came to the next fence. Bobcat was going like the wind; the fall hadn't done him any harm evidently, for they were gaining on Thunderer. Suddenly he realized with dismay that in his fall he had pulled the reins over Bobcat's head and that now they were both on one side of his neck. If the horse tried to run out at the next fence he would be helpless to prevent it.

He found his stirrups and crouched low, calling to Bobcat, "Give me a nice one, baby, right through the middle."

The big horse let out another notch and drove straight for the fence, rose in a tremendous leap, and landed flying.

"You're wonderful, baby. You're great!" cried the boy, his voice rising shrill in a frenzy of excitement, as they roared toward the next fence. "Just this one, boy! Take this one too, and I'll never forget it. You'll have carrots and apples, baby, baskets of 'em, boxes of 'em, barrels of 'em. Just this one! Now, boy, now!"

Bobcat let go with another long, driving arc and when they landed they were within five lengths of Thunderer.

"You're great, baby," cried Jack. "You're a bear cat! Let's give him a run for it, boy! We can't catch him, but we'll show 'em something!"

Now he was riding like a wild Comanche, his mouth wide open as his wild cheers urged the big chestnut to a fury of driving speed. They were closing fast on the black; they were at his flank—and Jack saw they were across the finish line. Two strides more and Bobcat drew past the tiring Thunderer.

Great waves of applause followed them as Jack eased up the big horse. "Listen, baby! That's all for you, boy!" Jack leaned over and patted the wet neck. "What a horse, Bobcat! Oh, what a horse you are! They'll never forget you, boy. They may forget who won, but they'll never forget who was second."

It was almost dark and the peepers could be heard through the soft April dusk. A slim figure was hurrying over the broad lawns toward the stable, carrying a small basket. As she entered the door the lights were switched on. Holley stood beside the door grinning broadly.

"Thought it was a thief, Miss Patsy. You forget something?"

Patsy hesitated. "I only thought I'd bring Bobcat some carrots."

"Wouldn't be twenty-two carrots, would it?"

"I suppose you're laughing at me, but it is."

"Why should I laugh?" asked Holley. "He just finished twenty-two I gave him. Superstitious we are, I guess.

But it don't hurt to stay on the good side of a fellow like that. Not too many of them around."

"I'm still all keyed up, Holley. Did you ever see anything like that run of his? Wasn't he grand?"

"That Bobcat!" said Holley softly. "That ole Bobcat! He's *somebody!*"

10

THE ROPING CONTEST

by STEPHEN HOLT

DES AWOKE as the first streaks of light slashed the cloudless eastern sky. Getting out of bed and favoring his right thumb, that "crunched" when he wiggled it, Des dressed gingerly.

"Not so good, thumb," he said softly, splashing water on his face and wetting down his dark hair. "But good or not"—he grinned wryly down at it—"you're the one I've got to win that calf roping with today."

Quietly he let himself out of the room, down the hall and stairs, then out the big front door. No El Gato lounging on the curb—that cookie was washed up. But, as he walked around the end of the *King's Hotel* and along the back street to the Economy, Des felt his heart squeeze shut. He almost wished El Gato did own Rocket. At least he was here, to be seen, maybe dickered with. He wasn't some mystery guy who might not show up at all —sending Rocket back to Mexico with Don Reyes.

Des walked through the barn door. Rocket nickered from his stall and began to prance impatiently.

A big lump in his throat, Des walked in beside him.

He couldn't breathe for the pain of thinking this might be the last time he'd saddle that big golden body.

"*Amigo,*" he whispered, rustling crushed oats and hay for the manger. "You've got to be good today—right on the calf, see?"

Rocket seemed to savvy. He stood quietly munching his oats as Des carefully saddled up, giving particular care to the condition of Rocket's back, seeing that no dust lay between the blanket and the saddle.

At last the big sleek horse stood ready for the contest ahead.

"Okay, *amigo,*" Des whispered, slapping Rocket's big thigh. "Eat hearty, you'll need it." Turning from the stall, he walked back to the main street and down it half a block to the *Hot Iron Cafe.*

"Eggs and bacon," he ordered, smiling sheepishly into the mirror in front of him.

"Gets to be a habit, pardner?" A voice beside him drawled. "Like partin' your hair."

Des turned and after a quick glance all but fell off his stool.

"Jim Fleet!" he exclaimed. Everybody knew Jim Fleet's tall gangly frame, his steel-blue eyes, that hint of a smile at the corners of a wide generous mouth. Des' heart began to hammer. He wished he hadn't run into him. Jim's time in the calf roping was twenty-one and two-fifths second—half a second behind El Gato's, but—

Jim grinned, studying Des' ever-present rope dangling from his arm.

"Let's see," he said, suddenly forgetting to eat the stack of hot cakes before him, and taking the rope from Des. "Boy!" He took both hands to the rope—big rawboned hands that handled the braided lariat with the deftness of a violinist with his bow. He turned to Des.

"It's kind of a funny thing to ask," he drawled. "But my rope's gone sour on me—if I could use this one, today?"

Des reddened to the roots of his sunburned hair. Wildly he stared around, trying to think of some excuse.— Finally, he brought his eyes back to Jim's.

"I'd sure like to—except that I'm using it myself."

Jim Fleet's eyes took in Des Harmon for the first time. Suddenly, they crinkled at the corners. "Sure enough— the kid Corporal Trenholm phoned in the last-minute entry for."

Des' jaw dropped. He'd intended doing that after breakfast. "Trenholm tended to it yesterday?"

Fleet nodded.

What happened after that wasn't quite clear to Des. He heard a lot of laughter from others lined up at the counter, and felt his rope slide back on his wiry arm.

And out on the sidewalk, he felt his neck. It had a big new silk bandanna around it—Jim Fleet's. And his words still sang in Des' ears. "Kid, here's something to give you luck." He'd been looking down at Des' swollen thumb.

Big Jim Fleet was a cinch to take the roping and the five-hundred-dollar prize. Even El Gato—well named The Cat, being so nimble with his hands—feared him. His voice from down the counter had sounded boasting, and as if trying to hide his fear, as he said, "Today, I hang up new record—maybe nineteen and two-fifths seconds, to tie the calf."

Walking back to Rocket, Des knew that the one thing he had to do was win. Win, or bust.

Bridling Rocket and leading him out of the barn, Des rode west till he came to the river. Dropping down the banks to the stream, he waded the horse out in it, waiting impatiently as Rocket drank.

A herd of cows and calves trailed slowly down to the water. Des pulled Rocket's reins and rode toward them, uncoiling his rope, making a small loop—one that a calf wouldn't jump through before he could jerk it shut.

A calf broke from its mother and skirted the riverbank.

"Okay, *amigo*." Des put the great gold stallion after him. It was a short race. The calf, frantic and bawling, was no match for Rocket's piston-like legs. In seconds, he was right on that flying ball of red fuzz.

Des, counting in what he thought was seconds, leaned out over his saddle and sent his rope singing through the air. A sharp pain shot through his thumb just as the rope left his hand. And he'd missed—the rope sailing off to the right, the calf scampering on to freedom.

It didn't matter that Des put Rocket in pursuit and, on the next throw, still counting the seconds, tied the calf in twenty-one and two-fifths seconds. One miss like that and the contest was lost.

"No ketchum prize that way," a faraway voice mourned, as Des loosed the calf and let it run bawling to its anxious mother.

Des jerked upright. His eyes went over the silent moody Indian boy sitting his pinto horse.

"White Cloud—what you doing here?"

"Watch you," White Cloud grunted. "You big chump think can win calf roping."

146

Des had that all figured out.

"Lynn come?" He asked. He could use a sight of that friendly face in the crowd this afternoon.

"Nope—send me," White Cloud said. His black eyes looked stolidly on Des as they might on a horse who'd eaten locoweed. "You know El Gato tie calf in twenty and two-fifths seconds—Jim Fleet plenty fast, too?"

Des nodded. He jumped clear off the deep end.

"I will tie calf today in nineteen seconds flat," he heard his voice say.

White Cloud shook his head. He was still shaking it as he rode with Des, out the graded road to the fair grounds through the contestants' gate and over to the big whitewashed plank corrals and bucking chutes.

The bucking-horse contest was on, now.

A white and pink horse rolled from the open chute bawling, trying to throw the puncher, who wore scarlet shirt and white chaps.

"From chute one—Rodgers on Pink Tea!" droned the announcer.

Des hoped Jim wouldn't be there right then. But he was.

"Howdy," he said, walking up. "How's the thumb, cowboy?"

Des managed a grin and moved it around. "Okay," he said.

He looked across the contest ground to the grandstand packed with people. They spilled out on the space in front. Indians wrapped in red-and-white striped Hudson's Bay blankets paraded around—their faces bright with paint; eagle feathers stuck in their jet-black hair.

Des' heart sank. There were Don Reyes and Jim Starr

and Nina. Des gripped his saddle horn to stay on. Then Rocket's owner hadn't shown up? For a second, Des thought of giving up. What was the use of winning the calf-roping money if it wouldn't buy Rocket. But staring at Reyes and Jim and Nina laughing and talking up there in the tenth row of the stands, Des knew that he couldn't quit. Something within him wouldn't let him quit.

He saw the pickup riders go out to lift Rodgers from Pink Tea. Heard the splash of applause for his ride.

For what seemed hours it went on.

Des couldn't think. Only that dumbness crept through him. His hand hurt.

"Bailey on Sudden Death! Sparks on Bean Shooter!" the loud-speaker system ground on. And finally with, "Rodgers wins the Bucking-horse Contest!" sputtered a moment, then blared, "Next event, the Cowboy Race— followed by the Pony Race. And then, the Calf Roping."

"That's us," Fleet said, climbing into his saddle. "First three winners in the Cowboy Race compete in the Calf Roping." He put spurs to his roan and danced out in front of the grandstand to the starting line.

"Yipee—Fleet!" roared the stands. Everybody knew Jim Fleet and Diamond, his roan rope horse.

"El Gato! The champion!" came next. A hush followed his entrance, then a buzz of excited talk.

Going over his record, Des grimly knew. He put Rocket's big golden head toward the half-dozen contestants and rode out on the track.

"Rocket!" a lone voice called. "Go to it, Rocket!"

That was Nina Starr, Des knew. His throat went dry. At least one person in the stands wanted him to win.

"Line up," the judges ordered.

The horses, prancing, their necks foamy under their manes, minced to the starting line.

Des kept Rocket's head pointed straight down the track.

"Easy, *amigo*," he whispered, straining his ears to catch the crack of the starting pistol.

Then suddenly it did explode.

A shout rose from the stands.

Des loosed Rocket's reins, giving him his head. The great horse, his powerful legs moving rhythmically, sped down the track, pulled away from the roan, from El Gato's black.

A gasp of sheer wonder burst from the stands.

"Rocket!" came from a thousand throats.

Des, his heart singing, rode him lightly, to the half mile, to the three-quarters, to where the finish tape loomed ahead, to where it looked as though Rocket couldn't lose.

Suddenly, the big horse swerved, turned in spite of all Des could do, and with the range instinct, rounded behind the horses sweeping to the finish line, and herded them across it—coming in last.

Des reddened, pulling Rocket to a halt. He heard the guffaws of laughter sweeping the stands and the loud-speaker blare, "El Gato on La Culebra wins. Fleet on Diamond, second; Rodgers on Midnight, third. Next event, the Indian Pony Race—followed by the Calf Roping for the championship of Western Canada."

Des rode Rocket slowly back to the corrals.

The bawl of calves filled his ears with an ache. His eyes stung with the alkali dust rising from their pound-

149

ing hoofs in the pens, as the punchers cut the roping calves into the "ready" chutes. This was the end. He'd lost the right to compete for the five hundred. Lost Rocket, for good, too.

El Gato rode by, sneering, "You lose horse, *si?*"

The loud-speaker confirmed it, after the hubbub of the Indian Pony Race: "Competing for the Calf-roping Championship by right of winning the Cowboy Race, El Gato on La Culebra, Jim Fleet on Diamond, and Roy Rodgers on Midnight," it blared.

Des got off Rocket and eased his cinch with aching hands. But suddenly his head spun around. What was that the stands shouted?

"The kid on Rocket! The kid on Rocket! Rocket! Rocket!"

The shouts went on and on, with Des wishing they would stop. He was a good sport. He could take losing —wasn't asking any special favors.

But it seemed he was to have no choice in the matter.

The loud-speaker crackled. The crowd hushed. And in the silence, dropping like a rock inside Des' head, plumbed the words, "By special request, an added contestant in the Calf Roping, Des Harmon on Rocket!"

The crowd went crazy. Yelling and shouting and laughing. Men slapping each other on the back—women laughing and nodding to one another.

And out by the corrals, Des gulped. He felt the sweat roll down along his back as he drew for position: First try, Rodgers, then Fleet, El Gato, and last of the four— himself. They were to have one calf each and three tries.

"*Si.*" El Gato smiled and winked at Des. "But one calf

missed—poof! The contest she is lost!" His beady black eyes bored into Des'.

Des turned away and walked back to Rocket. His hands could scarcely move as he loosened the saddle, moved it well forward on Rocket's back, then cinched it tight.

"Can't have it slip, *amigo,*" he breathed, softly.

Rocket's soft nose came down along Des' cheek.

It made a lump come into Des' throat, and a column of steel run along his back. It eased that pain inside him, and let him laugh at Rodgers' first calf, a little speckled thing that leaped from the chute and never gave Rodgers a chance to overtake it.

"Rodgers out—no catch," said the merciless loud-speaker.

Des gulped, and saw that Don Reyes had left the stands to take his place in the judges' booth—a little round raised house well out from the stands.

Fleet lined up, giving the gateman the nod.

His calf came—a black with a slow deceptive run.

Fleet overthrew, took a second shot and downed him.

"Fleet's time: twenty-nine and four-fifths seconds."

"Good for a second throw, that time," Rodgers said. "But second throws won't win here."

"*Sí!*" El Gato said. He touched his black lightly, as his calf, a rangy brindle, fled past the line. With a swirl of black on brown, he tossed his calf flat, leaped from his horse and tied the calf with a flourish, raising his hands in the air.

"Time, El Gato—twenty-three seconds, flat."

"Tie that," taunted El Gato, riding by Des.

Des barely nodded, his eyes on chute four. They saw

a red calf leap from it, then reach and pass the penalty line.

The whistle—for the roper to start.

Des put Rocket after the fleeing calf, leaning low, swinging his rope in short quick circles around his head.

The calf was fifteen feet ahead. Ten feet.

Des leaned over Rocket's ears and sent his rope, a live thing, out and down— He'd missed—no! He felt the rope sing taut on the saddle horn.

With a leap, he jumped down, followed the rope to the wriggling bawling calf. Two quick flips with his hands under the calf's foreleg and flank, a wind of his tie rope around its hind legs and one front one, and Des sprang erect, throwing his hands into the air.

"The kid—twenty-three seconds, flat," blared the loud-speaker.

"El Gato's time!" Des' heart bumped his ribs. He loosed his calf, coiled his rope and gently rode past the hazers, running the calf back into the chutes. "*Amigo*," he whispered to Rocket, "we are holding our own."

Rocket shook his head and blew out his breath.

The second round of calves started.

A shout that gave place to a groan rose from the stands as Jim Fleet missed his second calf, couldn't get his rope coiled in time, and watched its black body skip over the finish line.

"No catch—Fleet out," droned the announcer.

"It is you and me, eh, kid?" El Gato smirked, spring-ing lightly into his low flat Mexican saddle.

Des nodded, "Yes, you and me." The gate creaked open to let El Gato's second calf ooze through it.

"El Gato's time, second calf, twenty-one and two-fifths seconds," the announcer said, almost instantly. He said it as though he dared Des to equal it.

Des heard it through a fog. What was the use of trying any further? A panic struck him, feeling the big horse under him—the horse that would go back to Mexico prize money or no prize money.

But Rocket wouldn't let Des quit. The big stallion seemed to enter the game. He fairly smothered Des' second calf, a lean red bull, a moment after he catapulted from the chute and made it across the penalty line. In half a hundred leaping bounds, Rocket was on him, following his every corkscrew turn, till Des had only to reach down and drop the loop over the bullet head, then slip off and make the tie.

"Time, the kid, second calf: twenty-one and two-fifths seconds."

"No! It's crazy! Crazy!" roared the stands. "Timekeeper's crazy—two alike!" It had never happened. But it had.

Des made it back to the corrals, his knees like water.

"Kid, you've tied the world's record." Fleet grinned, lifting him to the dusty ground. "And with a bum thumb."

"But not a new one—watch. I tie my third calf in nineteen and two-fifths," El Gato boasted, piling into his saddle, his lithe brown hands coiling his rope for the final catch.

And he did just that, with the crowd going wild, and the white calf loping away after El Gato released him.

"El Gato's final calf," the announcer crowed. "Nineteen and two-fifths seconds—a new world's record."

Through the thunderous applause, El Gato sneered to Des, "*Gracias,* I can use that five hundred."

Des climbed into his saddle. His thumb hurt. Icy sweat ran down his back. He had a kink in his rope. And the calf, the color of dry grass, was leaping from the chute. It was over the line! And he hadn't even started!

But Rocket had. The golden horse reared and plunged for the calf. In less than fifty long fleeing leaps he was over it.

Des, his rope circling, leaned for the throw.

The calf dodged, turned back and—*under* Rocket's legs.

Des heard the stands gasp.

This was it. This was the end, knifed through his mind. It seemed as though life slowed for him, and he knew he felt Rocket's body under him for the last time.

Only force of habit, and the fighting instinct of a guy who wouldn't quit, made him lean low in his saddle, see the grass-colored calf come out the other side of Rocket, swing across and fling the loop.

He had the calf.

But the animal had dodged back under Rocket's belly. The rope was beginning to tighten. A warning, as from a bell rang in Des' head: "Rocket'll go crazy if that rope tightens and touches his belly!"

With a cry, Des leaped from the saddle and on the calf. He downed him before the rope pulled taut, flung him to the ground, and with his lariat tangled in his legs and those of the calf, made the tie. Up shot his hands into the air.

For what seemed an age, not a sound came from the breathless stands.

The loud-speaker, for once, seemed dumb.

Rocket's blowing came soft and free—the breathing of a horse with power in reserve.

Des felt the ice form around his heart.

And then, above the crack of a bronc's hoof on a coral plank, the announcer's voice welled out, "Ladies and gentlemen, a new world's record—nineteen and one-fifth seconds for Des Harmon. He wins the Calf-roping championship of the world."

Des heard the shouts from the stands as though in a daze. All he could see was Don Reyes coming slowly across the field—and Jim Starr and Nina.

Des released his calf, then turned to throw an arm around Rocket's sweaty neck.

"So long, *amigo*," he whispered, then turned to face Don Reyes.

"Oh, Des"—Nina's freckled face seemed alive with excitement—"you won! The calf roping, *amigo*, everything!"

Des stared. But of course she didn't understand. He met Don Reyes' eyes.

"Well, sir," he said, squaring his shoulders. "I see the owner didn't show up—here's your horse." He tried to hand Rocket's reins to Don Reyes.

"Oh, the owner didn't show up, eh?" Jim Starr stepped forward to take the reins.

Des looked from Jim's face to Nina's, then on to Don Reyes'. But Jim Starr's chuckle brought his eyes back to him.

"You, Rocket's owner?" Des faltered. His mind raced back to the morning on the river, when Rocket had seemed to know Jim Starr.

Jim grinned.

"Yep," he said. "And after what you did for me, who do you think owns him now?"

Nina's peal of laughter at Des' red face, and Reyes nodding rapidly and saying, "*Si, Si,*" told Des the truth. He protested. He said flatly, "He's your horse, Mr. Starr —just because you didn't get time to brand him that day down on the Rio de Sonora—" But all the time Jim was pressing the reins in his hands, and Rocket's big soft nose slid along his cheek.

Suddenly, Des' knees got weak.

"Mine, all mine," he whispered.

"Sure, all yours—and now you'd better go and collect your money."

Jim Starr lifted Des into the saddle and Des, with a flourish, rode over to the judges' stand.

"The kid! Rocket! The Palomino!" cheered the rapidly emptying stands.

Des rode up to the stand. He gently pressed Rocket's reins and the big horse reared high on his hindlegs, then dropped to the ground, and stood quiet.

The judge, George Roark, Jim Fleet's boss, stepped down and handed Des five one-hundred-dollar bills.

"Nice work, Des," he said.

Des pocketed the money, whispering, "Thank you," and Rocket dipped his head letting his silver foretop drop deep over his brown eyes. Des could have died for pride in him.

"Rocket! The Palomino!" came a final cheer, with spattering applause.

Des lifted Rocket's head high with a touch of the reins, gave him spur, and raced toward Nina and Jim and Don Reyes.

11

SUCH A
KIND WORLD

by MABEL LEIGH HUNT

OLD GRAY NELLIE was not a handsome horse. But in a kind world one does not need to be handsome in order to be loved. And the orphans at the Children's Home dearly loved Nellie. Since she was too old and stiff to work, Nellie's time was theirs. Being slow, she was safe for even the littlest ones to ride. And on that elderly, sagging back as many as six children could squeeze themselves in a merry row.

Privately, Nellie thought six riders were too many. "Three, now—" she wouldn't have minded at all. "But, by crickey, six squirming, kicking, screeching little orphans! Of course," added Nellie kindly, "they're too young and lively to know how it feels to be old."

And Nellie did have a great deal to be thankful for. Wasn't she spending her declining years in comfort? "An easy, idle life, with plenty of hay in my feedbox and plenty of love from the best sort of people, and that's kids," reflected Nellie. "Of course, not a *lavish* amount of hay. There could be more, if you come right down to it and state the facts plainly. But no one has any extras in a County Children's Home, so you're really a lucky old nag," Nellie told herself.

Imagine, then, what a shock it was to her, one cold December day, to look into her box and find it empty!

And, oh, the children felt almost as mournful as Nellie! For Mom Pickett, the matron, said, "It's too, too bad, but the time has come when we shall have to get rid of Nellie. There's no extra money to buy grain for an old horse that can no longer work for her board and keep. So," added Mom, before she thought how terribly shocking it sounded, "I'm afraid we shall have to sell Nellie for fertilizer."

"Sold down the river to the fertilizer plant!" ran the horrified whisper through the Children's Home.

The littlest orphans didn't understand, fortunately. But they heard that Nellie was doomed to go away because there was no food to be spared for her. They saved bits of crusts and apple cores, prunes, scraps of carrots, potato peel, cabbage leaves, and turnips and spinach, cooked and uncooked. Secretly and openly they carried these tidbits to Nellie, shivering in the damp December fields where she had been turned to nibble what little grass she could find. The poor old nag, growing more bony every day, was in no mood to turn up her nose and be choosy, though she found prunes hard to get down. And the cheese offered her in the sticky small palm of four-year-old Ruby McGlish made Nellie's mouth feel queer and gummy for hours. Oh, yes, it was a dismal time for all!

To make it worse, Mom Pickett said, "No more rides

on Nellie! A horse needs strength for that. Besides, the youngest ones must get used to doing without her."

"Maybe if you just mentioned Nellie—an' everything —to the Board," suggested Susan Spitznagle. Susan was thirteen. She had been in the Home a long time—long enough to know that in the hands of the Board of Directors rested the fate of orphans.

"I have a feeling the Board would decide, without a moment's prittle-prattle, that Nellie must go," answered Mom.

"Maybe if we'd drop hints around—to folks in town— and around," ventured Corky Trotter uncertainly.

"We could send an article to the *Bakersville Tattler!*" cried Mickey Malone, who was as smart as they come. "In the article we'd tell how hard Nellie used to work for the Home, and how we hate to see her go to the . . . oh, *you* know. How the little kids will cry for Nellie! It'd make folks feel awful sorry. Then they'd do something— maybe."

Mom Pickett smiled at Mickey. "It is a good idea," she murmured. "But there again I'm afraid the Board would think we were behaving in a way not expected of a Children's Home."

But Mickey and Corky and Susan and all the older children thought an item in the *Bakersville Tattler* ought to work magic. They couldn't give up such a promising idea.

"I could write the article myself," declared Susan, who was good in English composition. So, when Susan was not at school, or minding babies, or peeling potatoes, or wiping dishes, or dusting, or mending socks, she composed feverishly. Tears rolled off her small, freckled nose as she described with many vivid adjectives the plight of poor Nellie.

When she read the article aloud to the other children, her voice shaking, she could hear long-drawn sighs, sniffles, and choked sobs.

Even Mom Pickett was touched and said, "I do believe there is a future author among us—poor old nag!" Meaning, of course, that it was Susan who might some day become an author, not Nellie, the nag. "I declare," continued Mom, "it seems a pity not to see such a fine article published."

"Well?" queried the children eagerly.

"I'll call Mr. Cox, the president of the Board, and explain," promised Mom, seeing the hope in all the upturned faces. "If Mr. Cox says 'yes,' then the next time I go to Bakersville some of you may go along. You may take Susan's composition to the *Tattler* office and present it to the editor. But—if Mr. Cox says 'no,' then that will be quite another matter, you understand," warned Mom.

"Oh, please let Mr. Cox see how important Nellie is to us!" prayed the orphans at bedtime. So it was perfectly right and natural to them when Mr. Cox said "yes." Mom Pickett made an excuse to go to Bakersville the very next day, and with her, as Nellie's champions, went Susan and Mickey and Corky.

With thumping hearts the children entered the newspaper office. The editor, his hat on the back of his head and his pipe hanging on his lower lip, read Susan's composition, while the three orphans waited, tense and solemn-eyed. When the editor looked up, they could see twinkles in his eyes. He asked several questions, and with a thick blue pencil wrote across the margins of Susan's pages.

"By gravy, kids, this will make a spanking good story!" he said at last, with a slow grin. "Watch for Thursday's *Tattler*."

❋   ❋   ❋

"DO RIGHT BY OUR NELL," SAY KIDS AT COUNTY HOME
Campaign Now On To Provide Old-Age Pension For Beloved Old Nag

So ran the headlines in Thursday's *Tattler*. Oh, how the eyes of the orphans lighted up when they read these words and the article that followed! They could talk of nothing else. Happy as she was, Susan couldn't help feeling a bit disappointed that the editor had told Nellie's story in his own way, and not with Susan's lovely adjectives.

"Never mind, child," comforted Mom Pickett. "Editors are like that."

Susan forgot her disappointment in the flurry of events that followed. On the very next day the editor telephoned that the citizens of Bakersville had begun to contribute money for Nellie's groceries.

"We now have four dollars from the Women's Book Club, a dollar and ten cents from some town kids, and eight dollars from the Chamber of Commerce," said the editor. He sounded as excited as any gleeful orphan.

"That's thirteen dollars and ten cents for Nellie," cried Mickey, doing the sum rapidly in his head.

"Boy, oh boy!" exclaimed all the children, full of breathless admiration for everyone. For Mickey, because

161

of his lightning mental arithmetic; for the editor, because he was so definitely on their side; for Mom Pickett, because she was their only mother; for Nellie, *of course;* and for the Bakersville folk because of their kind hearts and giving hands.

Susan Spitznagle, carrying a turnip, and Ruby McGlish with a bit of cheese, pattered out to the field to break the good news to Nellie. The old nag pricked up her ears and turning her head politely aside, she let the cheese drop to the grass. "No more of that queer stuff for me!" snorted Nellie in a horsy undertone, though careful to thank little Ruby with a gentle nuzzling. "Nor prunes, nor turnips," added Nellie, "for my future begins to look brighter."

Indeed it did, for the following day an animal doctor came for the one and only purpose of checking Nellie's health. Mom called him a veterinarian, a word nobody could spell except Susan, and she got it wrong the first time. The doctor promised to give Nellie the best of medical care, *free of charge!*

"The old girl's pretty sound, for all her years," he assured the children. "What she needs most is rest, plenty of nourishing food, and at least three loving pats a day. I'll be around now and then to take her pulse and look at her tongue."

He gave Nellie a pill to show that he meant every word he said. It was huge. Corky Trotter and Mickey Malone promptly went into fits of laughter.

The children were still gazing fondly after the obliging doctor when the postman drove up, chuckling. Among the letters he left was one from New York addressed to Nellie the Nag, County Children's Home, Rural Route

3. When it was opened by Mom, two twenty-dollar bills dropped out! With the bills was a card bearing these words:

From an orphan who knew Nellie
when she and I were young.

Gracious! How perfectly thrilling to know that an orphan could go to New York and become prosperous enough to help out an old friend in need!

"Such things do happen to boys and girls who are good, hard-working and ambitious," declared Mom. "In fact," she went on, as if it were quite an ordinary, every-day thought, "there's nothing to hinder an orphan from becoming President. Or a great writer."

At that, the Home was so full blown with large, intense, round *Oh's* and *Ah's,* it was a wonder it didn't float off its foundations and soar skyward, like an inflated balloon.

Smiling farmers from at least three adjoining counties drove into the barnyard of the Home with corn and hay for Nellie. While these gifts were gathering, there came a photographer from one of the newspapers in the big city thirty miles distant. He took a picture of Nellie munching, with six orphans astride her. The photograph, which appeared in the newspaper's thick Sunday issue, was explained in large type:

ORPHANS SAVE AGED PET FROM FERTILIZER PLANT

It was the best thing in the paper, of course. There was Ruby McGlish, seated on Nellie's middle, looking squeezed but adorable. Susan Spitznagle perched proudly on Nellie's bony rump. Corky, a little blurry because of wiggling just as the camera's shutter snapped, clutched the mare's scraggly mane. The other three riders were grinning from ear to ear. And to the rueful surprise of Mickey Malone, only half of him showed, standing just inside the margin of the picture.

As for Nellie, crunching contentedly in her warm stall, another happy moment came to her when Mom Pickett said, "Nellie is getting fat and strong again, but the doctor said she must take life easy. So, from now on, children, only three at a time may ride her."

"Okay!" cried every cheerful little orphan.

"Okay, indeed!" exclaimed Nellie, under her breath. "Why, it's a dream come true!" And she reached for such a large mouthful of hay that it stuck out from her lips like cat's whiskers. "By crickey, I'm the luckiest old nag in the world, even if I did look every day my age and not at all handsome in that newspaper picture!"

Nellie stopped chewing and dropped her head humbly, for she was feeling very sentimental and deeply, deeply thankful. "In such a kind world as this," said Nellie, blowing softly through her nose, "one doesn't need to be handsome to be loved. And in my case at least, it all goes back to being loved by the best sort of people—and that's kids."

∘12∘

BUCEPHALUS: A KING'S HORSE

by ALICE GALL AND FLEMING CREW

"SAY NO MORE, Orestes. My mind is made up. The horse Bucephalus shall be sold."

It was on a summer day, more than two thousand years ago, that these words were spoken by Philonicus, a wealthy man of Thessaly in Greece. The two men, Philonicus the master and Orestes his slave, stood under a plane tree at one end of a green field in which a number of horses were pasturing. Around this field stretched on all sides the wide flat plains of Thessaly. And far to the north rose the lofty peaks of Mount Olympus, believed in those days to be the home of mighty gods who ruled the world.

Both master and slave were dressed in the long flowing robes of their time. But the master's robe was richly embroidered in silver, as were the sandals on his feet. About his thick brown hair he wore a band of purple. Philonicus was a man accustomed to being obeyed, and when he had spoken these words to Orestes he turned away.

But the slave put out a hand as though to detain him. "Master," he said earnestly, "there is not in all Greece another horse like Bucephalus."

"Well do I know that, Orestes," Philonicus answered, "and his new master shall pay a princely sum for him. I mean to sell him to King Philip of Macedon."

"King Philip of Macedon!" the slave repeated in amazement.

"None other," replied Philonicus. "King Philip knows horses. His army rides into battle mounted on splendid chargers fit for the war-god Mars himself. And it is said that Philip of Macedon would rather lose six Generals than one good horse of war. He will find use for Bucephalus."

"Master," Orestes pleaded, "you would not send Bucephalus into the cruel wars of Macedon? You know well how gentle has been his training. Never has he felt the sting of the lash. Surely, my master, you will not sell Bucephalus to King Philip."

"Such is my plan," Philonicus answered shortly, and a look of greed came into his eyes as he added, "King Philip's wars have brought him much wealth. His treasury is full. I mean to make him pay handsomely for Bucephalus." And with this Philonicus walked away.

After his master had gone Orestes stood looking sadly off toward Olympus. If only some god would help him save Bucephalus, he thought. But the great mountain seemed very far away and he, Orestes, was a slave. He could expect little help from the gods.

Presently he whistled softly, a long clear note, and in a moment or two Bucephalus appeared at the edge of a grove of oak trees far across the field. Trotting over to where Orestes stood, the beautiful dark bay horse lowered his head so that the slave might stroke his nose and pull his silky ears. For a little while he stood so, scarcely moving at all, and then suddenly he thrust his muzzle forward, gave Orestes a playful shove, and was off down the field like the wind, his head held high, his tail streaming straight out behind him.

This was a favorite trick of his and Orestes always expected it. But today the slave could not laugh; his heart was too heavy. From the time Bucephalus was a tiny colt Orestes had looked after him, feeding him and caring for him each day, and brushing his coat to keep it sleek and shining. It was Orestes who had put a bridle on him for the first time and taught him to carry a man on his back.

Bucephalus had not liked this. The bit hurt his tender mouth and having a man on his back seemed a strange thing. But Orestes had been so kind and patient that soon the strangeness wore off, and Bucephalus no longer rebelled but gladly carried the slave, mile after mile, across the broad flat plains.

Thessaly is a fair land, and for Bucephalus life was pleasant. There was the wide green pasture with its soft grass and its grove of oak trees where the shade was welcome on hot afternoons. And there was a stream of cool water where he drank when he was thirsty and in whose quiet pools he stood, knee deep, when the flies and insects annoyed him.

What would the life of Bucephalus be after this, Orestes wondered, as he watched the young horse galloping over the field? King Philip of Macedon was a powerful king, he knew, for the tales of his wars and

167

conquests had spread over all that part of the world. It was said that even now he was planning greater wars, that he longed to rule over a mighty empire, and dreamed of a day when all Greece should be his.

And now because Philonicus was greedy for gold, and King Philip of Macedon was greedy for power, Bucephalus was to have a new master!

On a morning late that summer King Philip of Macedon and his son Alexander, a lad of sixteen years, were walking through the palace gardens. They were on their way to the parade grounds to inspect the soldiers at their morning drill. But they had gone only a little way when they were met by a guardsman who saluted and stood at attention.

"Have you a message?" King Philip asked.

"Yes, Sire," the guardsman answered. "A stranger from Thessaly would see you."

"What is his errand?"

"Sire, he would sell you a horse," the guardsman told him.

"A horse!" King Philip thundered. "And you come to me with such a thing! Do you take me for a stable boy? This is an affair for some petty groom. If the horse is sound, let him be bought."

"The horse is a good one, Sire," the guardsman replied, "but the price is very high and the officers who are charged with such matters feared your displeasure."

"We have gold to purchase what we need," the king told him sharply. "Go, tell my men to use their wits."

"The price the stranger asks is thirteen talents, Sire."

King Philip looked at the guardsman in amazement. "Thirteen talents!" he exclaimed. "Why, such a price would scarce be paid for twenty horses! Dismiss the man at once. Tell him King Philip is no fool."

The guardsman saluted again and turned to go, but the boy Alexander called to him. "Wait, Simonides," he said. "The stranger comes from Thessaly, did you say?"

"From Thessaly," replied the guardsman.

"It is a land of splendid horses," Alexander said. "Let us have a look at him, father. Who knows? He may excel all horses in your stables even as you excel all other men in Macedon."

King Philip looked down at his son and laughed. "Yours is a sound head, my son," he said, laying his hand on the boy's shoulder. "Your words are well spoken. We shall see this stranger and his horse.

"Have this man of Thessaly bring his horse to the west riding field," the king told the guardsman. "And have trainers from my stables there, to put the animal through its paces."

When King Philip and young Alexander reached the riding field they found a number of the king's trainers already awaiting them.

"Where is this stranger from Thessaly and his horse?" the king asked impatiently.

"The Thessalonian comes yonder, Sire," said one of the men pointing toward the stables, "but the horse is being fed a measure of oats by the Thessalonian's slave."

King Philip laughed aloud. "What say you to that, Alexander?" he exclaimed. "A king must stand waiting while a slave feeds a horse!"

The boy Alexander made no answer for just then the Thessalonian, accompanied by a guardsman, came and knelt before the king.

169

"Rise, man of Thessaly," King Philip bade him. "Your land of Greece, beyond Olympus, is not unknown to me. I have seen its beautiful cities, its splendid temples, and its wide, fertile plains. A fine land it is. But tell me," he broke off, "what of this horse who now eats his measure of oats in my stables? I would know about him, for if he be worth but half the price you ask he must still be a wondrous horse."

"You shall see for yourself, oh King," Philonicus replied. "He is a mount the gods might envy you. I am asking thirteen talents for him, but were he yours you would not part with him for many times that sum."

"Do you hear that, Alexander?" the king asked, turning to his son. "What think you of the Thessalonian's words?"

"Why think of them at all, father?" the boy replied. "The horse himself will speak a truer tale than many words. See! Here he comes!"

From the stables across the riding field came the horse with the slave Orestes on his back. Alexander grasped his father's arm excitedly and the two of them stood looking in admiration. "He is indeed a splendid creature," exclaimed the king at last.

Bucephalus was quivering with nervousness. These were strange surroundings to him. Strange voices were all about him and he had eaten his oats in a strange stable, with men he did not know staring at him. He would have been badly frightened now if Orestes had not spoken to him encouragingly and patted his back.

"Look, father," said Alexander. "Do you note the fine slender legs, the long body, and the narrow, well-shaped head?"

"Ay," his father answered, and then turning to Philonicus he said: "You shall have your thirteen talents, unless my trainers find some hidden flaw in him."

Two of the trainers stepped forward and grasped the bridle, one on each side, while Orestes dismounted. He stood for a moment with his hand on the horse's neck. "A good friend you have been, Bucephalus," he muttered. "May the gods send just punishment on any man who dares mistreat you!" Then with a quick look at the two trainers the slave went over and stood at his master's side.

"Get on his back and put him through his paces," the king ordered one of his trainers.

But this was easier said than done. For when the trainer made ready to mount, Bucephalus jerked his head angrily and strained at his bit. The strength of the two trainers was barely enough to hold him. Suddenly he reared straight up on his hind legs, almost pulling the two men off their feet.

"Easy, Bucephalus! Easy, good horse!" called Orestes, and leaving his master's side the slave hurried forward. "I will quiet him," he said to the trainers.

"Stay where you are, slave!" King Philip ordered sharply. "I must learn this horse's temper before I send him to my stables." Addressing his trainers he commanded that Bucephalus be mounted without further delay.

But King Philip's trainers, expert horsemen though they were, were not equal to this task. Bucephalus lunged and reared, kicking and biting at them if they so much as spoke to him. At last the king waved his hand in a gesture of disgust. "Take him away!" he cried

171

angrily. "This horse is mad and altogether worthless. Turn him back to the slave. I would not give stable room to such a beast!"

The boy Alexander who had watched these proceedings with flushed face and flashing eye, now stepped quickly forward. "Wait!" he called, and with a scornful look at the two trainers he said in a loud clear voice so that all might hear, "What an excellent horse they lost for want of address and boldness to manage him!"

King Philip turned sharply on his son. "Do you reproach those who are older than yourself," he said, "as if you knew more and were better able to manage the horse than they?"

Alexander answered boldly, "I could manage him better than the others do."

"And if you do not," said his father, "what will you forfeit for your rashness?"

Alexander did not hesitate. "I will pay," he answered, "the whole price of the horse."

In spite of his annoyance the king could not help laughing at the boy's bravado. And the company joined in the laugh.

But Alexander went swiftly to the horse's head, and motioning the trainers away he took the reins in his own hands. At once he turned Bucephalus about so that he was facing the sun, for he had noticed that the horse was shying nervously at his shadow on the ground. Then, stroking the sleek neck, Alexander talked to Bucephalus gently.

Little by little the horse grew quiet. There was something in the touch of the boy's hand, something in the

172

He turned Bucephalus to face the sun

sound of his voice that gave Bucephalus confidence. He knew that here was someone he could trust.

With a quick leap Alexander was on the horse's back. Bucephalus threw his head up sharply and quivered with surprise. But his fear was gone. He pawed the ground, eager to be running free over the plain with this boy on his back.

And now Alexander spoke a word of command. Instantly Bucephalus bounded away and the boy did not try to stop him. Giving him his head he urged him to even greater speed. The king and his company looked on aghast, fearing that at any moment Alexander might be thrown to his death. But Orestes the slave smiled. "The lad has fine judgment with horses," he said. "Bucephalus is in good hands."

At last the horse slackened his pace and Alexander, turning him about, came back to the riding field, his face beaming with triumph. King Philip of Macedon was more proud at this moment than he had ever been before. This boy of sixteen was destined to conquer. The gods were with him!

Scarcely waiting for Alexander to dismount he threw his arms about the boy's neck and kissed him. "My son," he cried, "look you out a kingdom equal to and worthy of yourself! Macedon is too small for you!"

Little did King Philip think at the time how soon these words would come true. Little did he dream that within four short years his son Alexander, mounted on this same Bucephalus, would ride out of Macedon at the head of a great army which was to conquer half the world.

Four short years—how quickly they passed. As the days went by Bucephalus grew to love the boy Alex-

175

ander more and more. Eagerly he looked forward to those times when he could run, wild and free across the soft turf, the boy upon his back. This was what Bucephalus liked and it was what the boy liked. They understood each other, these two. They were friends.

But when the four short years were gone Alexander was no longer a carefree boy. He was a king. For King Philip was dead, leaving his dream of empire unfinished. His son Alexander must finish it for him. The young king's boyhood days were now over, he must turn to war and conquest. It was a hard task but he was ready.

One day there gathered on the parade ground a company of horsemen. They were no ordinary horsemen for they had shields and long sharp spears that glistened in the sunshine. These were fighting men.

A mighty cheer was lifted as young King Alexander approached mounted on his splendid horse Bucephalus. The fighting men lifted their spears in salute, and a moment later King Alexander and his army were on their way. Off they rode—to conquer a world.

Into far lands these Macedonians went. And always there was fighting and still more fighting. War! It was like a black cloud hiding the face of the sun. The world was turned into a world of hate and men forgot to be kind. There were years of hardship, suffering and bloodshed, but still Alexander's army marched on, conquering all before it.

King Philip's dream had come true, for Alexander was indeed the mightiest ruler in the world. His fame had reached into every land and wherever men talked of heroic deeds the names of the young king and his splendid horse were heard together. Alexander the Great and Bucephalus!

At first the horse had been frightened by the din of battle. The clang of weapons, the shouting of the soldiers, and the roaring and plunging of other horses round him had filled him with terror. But there was always the touch of his master's hand to quiet him, the sound of his master's voice to urge him on, and at last he grew accustomed to the tumult of war.

Through years of bitter fighting Bucephalus served his master well, carrying him triumphantly through battle after battle. And with each victory the ambition of King Alexander increased. With each new conquest that he made there came to him dreams of still greater conquest. He must go on and on, he told his men, until the whole world belonged to him.

But it takes a long time to conquer a world, and the life of a war horse is hard. There came a day when Bucephalus could no longer go into battle. He was growing old.

Alexander was forced to leave him in camp far behind the fighting lines. Here the faithful horse was well cared for and happy, and each day the king came and talked to him, and Bucephalus would lower his head so that his master might stroke his nose and pull his silky ears. And sometimes he would thrust his muzzle forward and give King Alexander a playful shove, as he had once done with Orestes the slave in Thessaly.

Back in Thessaly the horse Bucephalus was not forgotten, and tales were told of the days when he was a colt and carried Orestes over the wide Thessalonian plains. The same flat plains still stretched away, and

177

majestic Olympus, to the north, still raised its cloud-veiled summit. The years that had come and gone had brought little change to Thessaly.

"Orestes," said Philonicus one spring day, as again master and slave stood at the end of the green pasture, "do you remember the horse I sold for thirteen talents to King Philip of Macedon?"

"Yes, master," answered Orestes. "I shall not forget Bucephalus."

"Who would have dreamed," went on Philonicus, "that one day he would become the most famous horse in all the world? He is now almost as famous as the great Alexander himself."

"Bucephalus was always a good horse, master," Orestes said simply.

"Ay, a good horse," Philonicus repeated, turning away. "And thirteen talents was a good price, too. A handsome price, Orestes."

For a time the slave stood silent, and then walking slowly he went through the green pasture toward the little grove of trees. Midway of the field he paused and looked off at Mount Olympus. "A handsome price indeed," he said softly. "But if you had been mine, Bucephalus, not all the gold in Macedon could have bought you."

°13°

MOHAWK MAKES A COMEBACK

by C. W. ANDERSON

THREE WEEKS had passed since Mohawk had limped out of the van and into his new home. He now moved much more easily, and the swelling in his leg was almost gone. The trainer had sent instructions for his treatment, and Peter spent all his spare time putting cold bandages on the injured leg. Every day he took Mohawk down to the brook to stand for a long time in the cool, flowing water. This was very good to take the soreness out of a muscle or tendon. The soft yielding meadow was very pleasant to a horse whose legs had become sore from many years of racing over hard tracks, and soon he began to have a spring in his walk.

Although Peter was still very fond of Ned and Brownie his feeling about Mohawk was different. Not only because this was his own horse, but because he was so intelligent and gentle and sensitive that Peter found it hard to leave him, even for a short time. Mohawk seemed to miss Peter just as much, for he was always standing with his head over the stall door waiting for

him to come back. For a shy boy who had few play-
mates it was an ideal companionship.

One day several weeks later Peter's father stood watching Mohawk as Peter led him back from the brook.

"I think you could start riding him a little now," he
said. "He isn't limping at all, and you're very light. I'll
see if I can borrow a saddle and bridle from the Wash-
burns. They have no saddle horse now, so they don't use
them."

Peter had never ridden except on Ned's or Brownie's
wide back; but he had read everything he could find
about riding, and he had no fear of horses. He felt sure
that Mohawk would know he was learning and try to
help. For so long, now, he had been riding in his dreams
that he did not feel like a beginner at all.

When Peter's father saw how Mohawk opened his
mouth to take the bit, and lowered his head so that Peter
could reach to put on the bridle, he said that he would
never worry about Peter's safety with such a horse. Then
the saddle was put on and tightened, and Peter proudly
led Mohawk out of the stable. His father helped him into the saddle, and as Peter gathered up the reins he felt
that the great moment of his life had come. He was
riding his own horse.

They started off for the meadow, where the footing
would be soft, and now Peter realized the difference between the walk of a saddle horse and a work horse.
Mohawk's was so smooth and springy it was like flowing
water; and when he pranced a little because he felt so
gay, Peter tingled from head to foot. Certainly nothing
in the world was as fine as this.

As they crossed the brook and went into the pasture

beyond, Peter was surprised to find how natural it felt to be in the saddle. When they came back to the stable an hour later no one, seeing how easily he sat his horse, would think that this boy was coming back from his first ride.

The second week they were going longer distances, and there was no sign of soreness in Mohawk's leg. They were still going only at a walk, to give the leg a chance to become strong and supple before trying a faster pace. This was the best possible thing for Peter also. Each day he was feeling more at home in the saddle and in rhythm with Mohawk's every movement. Most beginners are so anxious to start galloping that they are impatient of any details, and as a result they usually do everything a little wrong afterward.

It was enough for Peter just to be with his horse; he would have been happy to ride at a walk for months if necessary. There were so many things to remember: the heels down, the knees gripping just so, the hands light and firm on the reins. To Peter, who wanted perfection in this above all else, no detail was too small or unimportant.

Coming back across the meadow one day, Mohawk began prancing very lightly, then a little faster, and in a moment he was in a trot. At first Peter sat close to the saddle; then as he felt the trot lengthen he found himself rising a little with the rhythm of it, and soon he was in perfect unison with the gait.

It had seemed wonderful before, but now Peter saw life stretched out before him in a succession of golden days. He rode up to the kitchen door and called to his mother excitedly. She came out to watch and was really surprised to see how well Peter rode. When they came back from their circle of the farmyard Mohawk stopped expectantly. He was a great favorite with Peter's mother and knew she would always have something for him: an apple or a carrot or a lump of sugar; sometimes even a cooky, which he liked especially.

Needless to say, Mohawk received more care than most horses get. His coat was brushed many times a day until it shone like burnished metal in the sun. His mane and tail were dark and silky, and he carried his head in such a spirited way that he was a very handsome sight. No one in the countryside had ever owned anything like him, and the neighbors always stopped work to see him go by.

The crispness in the air acted as a tonic on Mohawk; he pranced and seemed overflowing with energy and spirit. Peter now rode at a canter as easily as at a trot, and sometimes when they came to a stretch of smooth road he would let Mohawk go at a fast gallop if he wanted to. Speed was what Mohawk had been bred for, generation after generation; so it was only natural that he should remember his racing days and sometimes like to hear his feet drumming and feel his mane flying. To Peter it was very thrilling.

All through the winter there was scarcely a day when Peter did not take Mohawk out for a ride after school. Even snow and cold did not stop them; for Mohawk had his heavy winter coat, and he always seemed pleased and surprised at the strange white world outside.

When the buds were showing on the trees again, Peter and Mohawk understood each other as horse and rider seldom do. The reins were hardly necessary; Mohawk responded to Peter's voice, even in the excitement of galloping at full speed.

As the hills and meadows grew greener and the days lengthened, Peter and Mohawk went farther and farther over the countryside. Nearly all errands were done on horseback. If Peter's mother needed something from the store in the village a few miles away, it seemed they had been gone only a few minutes before she heard Mohawk's neigh outside as he waited to be rewarded. By the time summer had come there was scarcely a road or trail within ten miles that they had not explored.

The muscles under Mohawk's shining coat stood out clear and sharp and rippled and flowed as he moved. Peter's father said he had never seen a horse in finer condition. Often on a Saturday, after he had done his chores, Peter would put a sandwich in his pocket and go out with Mohawk for all day.

He had never realized before how many wild animals were near by. Several times they came upon startled deer and were thrilled to see the long graceful bounds that carried them over the highest walls with ease. Occasionally a fat woodchuck would scurry away with his awkward, waddling gait; often they saw pheasants and partridge, and once a fox that vanished so quickly and completely that Peter was not sure whether he saw or imagined it.

There were chores to be done each day, and Peter often helped in the fields with work that was not too heavy for an eleven-year-old boy. But there was always time for riding too. Peter's father realized that his son's interest in horses was much more than a childish enthusiasm, so he encouraged him to learn as much as

183

possible about them. He was wise enough to realize that a person may accomplish more in the direction of his interest than in any other.

The small bookshelf in Peter's room was now almost full of books about horses, and all of them had been read many times. Whether it was the record of his hero, Man o' War, or the best way to treat a cracked hoof, it all stayed clearly in his mind.

In late July the papers were full of news of the opening of the Saratoga racing season. One day Peter noticed the name of Mr. Harley, the trainer who had given him Mohawk. He was at Saratoga with horses he was training for the races there. Peter felt that he had never thanked Mr. Harley for Mohawk, and he wished for a long time that he could show the trainer how well Mohawk was. He told his father about it and asked if he could ride over the next day. It was only ten miles away, and since the training track was in the outskirts of the city there would be very little traffic early in the morning. His father gave his consent, and Peter spent all the afternoon grooming Mohawk and cleaning and polishing the saddle and bridle.

The moon was pale in the sky, and only a faint pink glow showed in the east when Peter dressed next morning. He hurried down to the stable to feed Mohawk, and then came back to eat the breakfast which his mother had set out for him the night before.

By the time he had brushed and saddled Mohawk it was quite light. They had the road to themselves, and mile after mile was quickly covered by Mohawk's long swinging trot. Before Peter realized it they were in the outskirts of Saratoga. Soon the Oklahoma Training Track loomed ahead, and they could hear the galloping of horses. Mohawk's head went up and he sniffed the air, pranced, and blew loudly through his nostrils. There was no doubt that he remembered the old scenes well and that the spirit of competition still flamed strong in him.

Peter rode through the gate and into a very colorful and exciting scene. Half a dozen horses were on the track galloping, while many others were being led around and cooled after their workouts. The rail of the track was lined with grooms who had colored blankets over their arms, exercise boys in breeches and boots, and trainers who were timing their horses. A chestnut horse and a gray came galloping by, head and head, at almost racing speed. Mohawk kept snorting and prancing; he wanted to be racing with them.

When Peter could take his fascinated eyes off the horses he began to look for Mr. Harley. Soon he saw him talking to a man, and he waited near by. As the trainer turned around he caught sight of Mohawk; then he walked over and looked more closely. Peter could see how surprised he was.

"Why, Mohawk, old-timer, I wouldn't have known you," he said as he patted his nose. "How did you do it, Sonny?" he said to Peter. "He never looked any better, not even in his younger days."

Peter told all about it, and the trainer nodded his head as he studied him.

"You like horses," he said. "You'll be a real horseman someday."

This was the greatest praise possible, and Peter flushed with pleasure.

Mr. Harley looked Mohawk over thoroughly and ran

his hands over his legs. "He's sound as a dollar and hard as nails. He could step out and win a race tomorrow." He stopped suddenly, looked Mohawk over again sharply, then turned to Peter.

"What would you rather have than anything else?" he asked. "If you had the money to get it, what would it be?"

"A colt," said Peter. "A colt that I could take care of, that might grow up to be famous."

The trainer smiled. "That's what I've been wanting too, for a long time," he said. "Once I thought I had one, a really good one." He seemed to be talking to himself. "If only Black Bart had had the courage and honesty of old Mohawk here, I would have had one. But who knows? You may have the luck. . . . I'd like to see how Mohawk goes," he said after a moment. "Do you gallop him at a fast pace?"

Peter nodded.

"Take him over to the quarter pole, that red and white one, and let him run down to me here at top speed."

Mohawk danced up the track proudly Here he was again; this was something he knew and liked. When Peter turned him around he started at once without urging, and the wind whistled in Peter's ears. He had never realized before how fast Mohawk could really run. When they came back to Mr. Harley he was putting his watch in his pocket.

"The yearling sales start next week," he said. "With five hundred dollars you could buy a real nice colt. Mohawk can win a race that will give you a purse of that amount. He's been away from the races for a year and is supposed to be all through, so the handicapper will let him in with a very light weight. I'll get a jockey to ride who has handled him many times and is very fond of the old fellow. What do you say?"

"I'll have to ask my father," said Peter in a low voice. "You—you're sure he can win?"

"He'll win," said Mr. Harley. "He has stamina, and he never quits. I'll pick a race where he'll have a great chance. Mohawk should have been a topnotcher, but he didn't have quite enough speed. He has everything else." He patted Mohawk's nose. "How about it, old-timer, want to run once more?"

Mohawk rubbed his head up and down against the trainer's shoulder as if in assent.

°14°

THE CUTTER RACE

by STEPHEN MEADER

B UD GOT up at four-thirty and dressed, in the bleak dark of that Washington's Birthday morning. The cold and the excitement made him shake all over like a leaf as he went stumbling out into the barn. But he climbed the mow and dug into the hay savagely with the fork to pull himself together. And when he came down Tug was there to give his hand a warm, reassuring lick.

The white terrier was all but well now. Only a few healing scars remained from his encounter with the gypsy dogs, and his limp was entirely gone.

Bud hustled through the work in time to give Cedar a last brushing down, then fed and watered him with care and went in to breakfast. For Aunt Sarah's sake he made a valiant effort to eat, but he was keyed too high that morning to enjoy the taste of food. Uncle John came out with him to help harness, and by eight o'clock they were ready to start. Bud waved good-by to Aunt Sarah and drove the colt out of the dooryard to the musical jingle of bells. Tug went too, sitting erect between their feet.

All down the snowy miles to Riverdale Bud had to

189

check Cedar's pace, soothing him constantly by voice and hand, for the colt felt like skylarking.

"This jog to town is a good thing fer him," Uncle John said. "It'll take some o' the devilment out of him, an' maybe he'll be ready fer business at race time."

At the outskirts of the town they overtook the Hunters' sleigh, in which Cal and his father were riding, and accompanied them to the speedway. There was still nearly an hour before the first heat was scheduled to begin, and Bud blanketed the colt and walked him slowly up and down while the others were getting their tickets for the grandstand. Uncle John reported his injury to the race committee and made the necessary arrangements for having a substitute drive in his place.

The holiday had brought out a far larger crowd than had been present the afternoon before. Not only had many come afoot, but there were rows of cutters ranged along the sides of the track, with an occasional automobile among them. The sky was overcast and the air sharply cold.

"Looks as if it might snow later," said Uncle John, casting a weatherwise eye aloft. He had come back for a last look at Cedar before the race.

A gong began to clang at the judges' stand. "Ten minutes," said Uncle John. "Warm him up a bit back here, then take him up over the course so it won't be strange to him. Good-by, lad."

Bud took Cedar's blanket off and let him stretch his legs a trifle on the road back of the stand. When he seemed well limbered up the boy swung his horse to the foot of the speedway and jogged him up past the grandstand. Then along the line of jingling sleighs and pungs he guided Cedar toward the starting-point. There were laughter and a few jeers as they passed—the strong young horse, with his winter coat as smooth as Bud could brush it, but looking a bit rough and uncouth about the legs; the scarred old cutter, its moth-eaten cushions well dusted and its steel runners polished till they gleamed; and sitting very straight under an ancient buffalo robe, the serious-faced boy with his eyes to the front.

Eight horses besides Cedar were moving up to the start. Most of them were local trotters. They had beautiful, clipped legs, and right at their tails—on them, in fact—sat their drivers, in sulky sleighs that were no more than light skeletons of braced steel, with ridiculous little shells of seats above.

As they swung into position Bud looked off down the mile straight-away with a pounding heart. He felt himself in a sort of daze, his arms heavy, helpless. Then almost before he knew it the starting gun had sounded. Ahead of him flew the other eight, close-bunched.

A laugh went up as the boy gritted his teeth and urged the sorrel colt after them. Hot tears of anger filled his eyes. But the swift rhythm of Cedar's haunches under the taut reins brought back his confidence and even a thrill of pride. He steeled himself for the job ahead.

And now from the crowds that lined the snow path came scattering cheers as they went by, for some of the men from the upper end of the county and some of Bud's schoolmates recognized them. Slowly, very slowly, it seemed to the boy, they were coming up—overhauling first one rival and then another, till, as the wire drew close, there were six behind them.

Cedar finished in third place. Bud swung him around

191

to pass the grandstand on the return journey. He could not bring himself to look up. He was red with shame. But there were many good horsemen along the track who had seen the colt's fine spurt and who threw Bud a word of encouragement as he went back for the second heat.

Well, there should be no leaving at the post this time! Bud gathered the reins, and the sorrel picked up speed as he neared the start. Over the line he went like a shot, right abreast of the leaders. Halfway down the track Bud looked sidewise. The winner of the first heat, a game little chestnut gelding named Billy D., was holding even with the boy's sleigh seat, trotting with all that was in him. The rest were trailing behind. Bud thrilled to see the red colt then. As his grip on the reins tightened, Cedar responded, speeding faster and faster, with the wind in his mane, over the hard-packed snow he loved. And he crossed the finish line with a good three lengths to spare.

There was a yell from the crowd as the time went up. Bud looked at the board and nearly choked with surprise. Two-eight, it said. Surely there was a mistake. In a minute they would find it out and change the "0" to a "1." But no, the crowd was still cheering. "Cedar! Cedar!" cried the voices in the stand, hailing a new popular favorite. And flushed this time with pride, Bud grinned up at the throng, trying to find Uncle John and Cal and Tug.

The colt was over his first nervousness now, and Bud let him take plenty of time in going back for the final test. When they reached the start the boy got out of the sleigh and stooped to rub down Cedar's steaming legs with a dry piece of sacking. A man spoke, so close to his shoulder that it startled him.

"Give 'im the whip, this last heat," he said in a low voice. "They're goin' after yuh. That colt's got better time in 'im, yet, an' you'd better use it. Don't look around, but drive like the devil, all the way!" And the man was gone before Bud could open his mouth to reply. The single glimpse he got of him had shown a sallow, thin fellow with a black mustache, wearing a great coonskin coat.

Already the horses were back on the track. Bud was thinking quickly, disturbed by the uncalled-for advice of the stranger. It was true enough that he must do his best to win this last heat, but why had the man been so anxious to tell him so? Was he betting on Cedar? Uncle John's words came back to Bud as distinctly as if he were hearing them spoken: "Don't let anybody tell you how to do. Drive your own race." And the boy resolved that, green as he was in such matters, he would use his own judgment and disregard all outside counsel. Still worrying a little, he swung the big red colt into place above the start.

Down they came, all together, like a cloud before the wind, as the flag dropped.

Cedar was rocking along, smoothly as ever, almost in the center of the group. Suddenly Bud saw two horses moving up, one on each flank, and though less than a quarter of the course was finished their drivers were plying the whip savagely. As the sleighs drew even with Cedar's head both men pulled inward a barely perceptible distance. The colt's flying forefeet were very near to striking their runners.

In another instant he might have broken, for he was

193

disconcerted and tossed back his head. But Bud pulled him far off to the left and spoke to him once or twice as Uncle John would do. The young pacer held his stride and a second later was going again like the wind, outside and nearly abreast of the others.

Beyond the half mile they had passed all but the little chestnut, Billy D. He fought them hard all the way down, but Cedar's mighty strength was too great a handicap. Bud was slacking off on the reins at the finish, and the colt drifted easily under the wire, a length to the good.

The spectators came pouring out of the stand as Bud guided Cedar off the track. A crowd of curious men and boys surrounded them, staring open-mouthed at the young stallion while Bud wiped down his legs and blanketed him. After a moment Uncle John shouldered through the onlookers, followed by Tug and the Hunters. No words were needed to express the farmer's joy. It glowed in his square, brown face.

"That was drivin', boy!" he said, and gripped Bud's hand. Then he looked around at the crowd. "Here, let's git the colt out o' this an' give him a chance to rest," he added.

In the lee of a pine thicket near the upper end of the speedway they found a sheltered place to tie the horses and eat their lunch. When Cedar was cool enough they gave him a light feed and a little drink.

"What was it happened up there near the start in the last heat?" asked Uncle John as they consumed Aunt Sarah's sandwiches and pie.

"Two of the drivers tried to box me," said Bud, and he went on to tell how Cedar had escaped from the trap.

194

"There was another funny thing happened," the boy remarked. "Just before the last heat a man came and warned me to drive for all I was worth and lay into the colt with the whip. Do you suppose he really meant to help me? I didn't like his looks, so I didn't pay much attention to him."

"He might've wanted Cedar to win," said Uncle John, "but it sounds more to me as if he'd been tryin' to use the colt up—kill his speed fer this afternoon. Who was the feller?"

Bud described the stranger, but neither Uncle John nor Myron Hunter could remember having seen him.

The next two hours were hard for the youthful jockey. No one talked much. They all took turns at leading the blanketed pacer up and down to keep his legs from stiffening. Now that the first flush of winning the elimination race had passed, Bud had moments of bitter doubt. He thought of the crudeness of their preparations for the final and compared them mentally with what was going on in the big, steam-heated box stalls at the hotel stable, where grooms and trainers were even then putting the last fine touches on Chocorua and Saco Boy.

He thought of Cedar—a raw young colt, driven down that forenoon over ten miles of country road, raced in three hard heats in the morning, and handled clumsily by an amateur driver. What chance had he to win against those famous pets of the racing-game, fresh from a night's rest and maneuvered by wise and tricky hands?

Then he looked up at the big red horse stepping proudly along at his side, saw the courage that glowed in his eye and the strength of his arched neck—and shame

195

filled the boy's heart. Cedar, at least, had no yellow streak.

Two o'clock came, and the young pacer was put back between the shafts of the cutter. Uncle John pulled the last buckle tight with his left hand and gave the colt's cheek a lingering pat. "I guess it's time to go down to the judges' stand," he said. "They'll likely make the three hosses parade past 'fore the first heat."

They led Cedar down the track, still in his blanket, as far as the upper end of the grandstand. There the wraps were taken off and Bud took his place once more in the sleigh while the others climbed to their seats in the pavilion.

There was a great throng gathered at the track that cold, gray afternoon. The Governor had come over from Concord, and by his side in the decorated box loomed the gigantic figure of a famous New Hampshire Congressman who never missed a good harness race if he could help it.

Driving up past the crowds to the judges' stand, Bud realized with dismay that he and Cedar were a part of the spectacle that these thousands had come to watch. Luckily his stage-fright did not pass through the reins into the horse. He was as gay as ever, and even danced a little as the band played.

Close by, their blanketed forms the center of deep knots of men, were the colt's two opponents. Bud watched them as their coverings were stripped off. Saco Boy stood forth magnificent—a great black stallion with fire in his eyes and mighty muscles leaping in his neck and shoulders. He was more massive and even taller than Cedar, but, Bud felt, no better proportioned.

Then his glance shifted to Chocorua. Instantly the old hatred he had felt when he first saw her returned. It seemed as if no horse had a right to such slim, long racing shanks. She was built like a greyhound, and the similarity was made more striking by her blue roan color and the clipped smoothness of her chest and legs. Her head was long and narrow and wicked. With her ears back she was like a reptile—venomous.

As Bud looked past her his eye was caught by a coon-skin coat and a thin, dark-mustached face above it. It was the stranger of the morning, standing close by the mare's head and engaged in an earnest conversation with two men. One was a hard-faced, smallish man in black furs—Andy Blake, the mare's driver. The other was Sam Felton himself. The fat-jowled magnate's eye met Bud's and flashed with recognition. Was it Cal who had said that the Feltons never forgot a grudge? There was some-thing of vindictive triumph in that glance that the boy did not like. And the mystery that had puzzled him was cleared up at last. Instead of a friend the man who had given him the tip was an enemy—one of Chocorua's backers. No wonder he had urged Bud to drive the colt to a needless whipping finish in the morning race. Perhaps it was he who had engineered the attempt to box Cedar, as well. The boy thanked his stars he had followed Uncle John's advice.

From the judge's booth sounded the sharp, impatient banging of the gong. "Ten minutes!" came the call, and Bud gathered the reins once more for action.

Bud took Cedar on a little warm-up spin along the track, then came back with the others to the judge's

197

stand. There was another laugh at the rude racing turn-out from Red Horse Hill, for many people in the crowd had not been present that morning. Andy Blake, mounted close behind the tall hind-quarters of his mare, grinned spitefully at Bud's reddening face. But old Billy Randall, who held the reins over Saco Boy, gave the lad a friendly nod.

"Sorry 'bout John gittin' hurt," he said, "but you drove a good race this mornin'. That's a great youngster you've got there."

From the judges' stand the horses' and drivers' names were read out and the conditions of the race announced. Three heats were to be driven and the championship decided on points if no horse won twice. As the announcer put down his megaphone a babel of sound rose from the stands—cheers and shouts of encouragement. The three drivers turned their horses' heads and jogged slowly up the track toward the start.

Bud had an entirely different feeling from the one with which he had entered the morning race. He was alert and tense now, determined to fight. They swung around at the head of the snow path and got under way. Nearing the start the big, black trotter flashed out ahead, fiercely impetuous. He left the line a good four lengths beyond the others, and Bud expected to hear the jangling of the recall bell. Instead came the report of the gun, and the starter's flag fell. In spite of an outcry from the crowd and the wild gesticulations of Andy Blake the heat was on.

A great excitement entered Bud's veins. His grip on the reins tightened, and he shouted to Cedar through the whipping wind. The colt was pacing swift and sure as in the forenoon, one pointed ear cocked back for Bud's voice, the other forward. Chocorua's evil head, close by their sleigh-seat at first, dropped back and back till Bud could see her no longer, and the colt drew up little by little on the great trotting stallion.

It was such a finish as horsemen dream of. Scarcely half a length apart down the last quarter fought the sorrel and the black. There was so little to choose that many called it a dead heat. But with the sting of Randall's whip on his shining side, Saco Boy flung himself under the wire a nose ahead.

"Two-five and a quarter!" bawled the timekeeper. And as Bud came out of the spell of the race he realized that thousands of voices had been calling on Cedar to win.

Again the long mile back to the starting-point, and then a little breathing-spell as they got ready for the second heat. Blake, sullen and resentful, had saved his mare after the uneven start. She stood there, poised on her slim legs, hardly breathing as yet, while the black stallion puffed and pawed and flung white spume flecks back over his ebony neck. Cedar was quieter, but the exertions of the day had begun to tell on him. His deep sides rose and fell with the effort he had made. Bud soothed him with pet names and rubbed him unceasingly as they stood waiting.

It had begun to snow when the starter called them out —long, slanting darts of white hurled across the track by the keen north wind.

They brought their horses to the right about and came down to the post again. The tall roan mare leaped to the front this time, with Randall and Bud driving close at her heels. Blake was not lagging now. From the start he drove her—drove her with hard hand and hard voice, the whip ever poised above her lean back. And still, as she fled away, came Cedar after her, eager as a hawk, his swift feet thudding on the firm-packed snow. Off to the right the great black horse held the pace for a while, then burst into a thunderous gallop, and they left him and sped on.

It was a terrific gait the mare was making. And she held it to the end, for Blake began using the whip at the three quarter-post and brought her in under a flying lash. Gallantly Cedar followed, but at the finish there was still a length that his weary legs could not make up.

Bud had to shut his jaw hard, for he wanted to cry as he stood by Cedar's side after that second heat. There was a faint, constant trembling in the steel muscles under the colt's damp hide and his coat was bright no longer, but dark with sweat. Rubbing and working at those beautiful legs as if his life depended on it, the boy talked to him breathlessly, pleading with him, begging forgiveness for the one last trial that Cedar must endure. Twice he had given his best and lost. The race and the purse were gone, of course—utterly beyond their reach, but Bud knew they must keep on and see it through.

When he looked up for a moment men were jumping in the air in excitement, shouting and pointing toward the judges' pavilion. On the board were figures which at first Bud read without believing. They said: "2.04."

Then at his elbow he saw Billy Randall standing. The old trainer's voice was queer and husky as he spoke.

"I wanted to look at that colt o' yours, lad," he was saying. "I guess we're through—Saco Boy an' I. Once he breaks in a race he's done for the day. But you've got

The colt's great heart responded

the greatest snow horse in New England there under that blanket—"

"Ye're durn right!" interrupted a voice behind them, and Bud turned quickly to see Long Bill Amos. "The finest pacer I ever see!" continued the teamster. "An' if you don't beat that roan she-devil—now—" He choked. "Look at her! By gosh, I didn't come all the way from Boston to see this colt get trimmed."

Bud looked at Chocorua. There she stood, ears back and head hung low, her eyes rolling wickedly at the grooms who toiled over her legs. She was fresh no longer.

Randall nodded at Bill in full agreement.

"Now look here, boy," said the veteran driver to Bud. "It would ruin some horses to give 'em the punishment that Cedar's takin' today. But I know him. Know his blood. Know his trainin'. He'll stand it. You beat the mare an' you've *won!*"

"Wh-what?" Bud gasped.

"Sure!" put in Amos. "It'll be decided on points. Take a look at that board, front o' the judges' stand."

Bud's eye followed his pointing finger, and a gust of hope swept through him. The board on the pavilion read:

	First Heat	Second Heat	Third Heat
SACO BOY	1	3	—
CHOCORUA	3	1	—
CEDAR	2	2	—

To put a figure "1" after Cedar's name in the third heat would give him a first and two seconds, while the best either of the others could make would be a first, a second, and a third.

With Long Bill helping him, Bud bent down and re-

203

doubled his efforts on the colt's legs. As he worked he whispered to the brave young horse, over and over, that this time he *must*, and he felt Cedar's soft lips fumbling playfully at his ear.

The stand was in an uproar when the red colt and the roan mare went back for the final heat. But through the shouting Bud heard a deep, familiar bark and looked up to see the white terrier between Uncle John and Cal. The farmer was bent forward, his face gray and strained, and Cal was giving vent to shrill yells of encouragement. Bud waved a stiff mitten and went on as if in a dream.

Driven whirls of snow were cutting their faces as the jockeys turned above the start once more. Men along the track were huddled close together for warmth and thrashing their arms to shake off the numbness. It was blowing hard, and Bud knew the temperature must be near zero.

There were only two of them left to race, for Saco Boy had been withdrawn. Bud looked down the track through the white storm that hid the far-off grandstand and the town. The wind had swung to the northeast now, and into it they must go. The boy gathered the reins. Cedar's red haunches quivered into action. For the last time they crossed the starting-line.

How they got down to the half-mile post Bud never knew. The air was full of white, and snow particles bit at his eyelids, half blinding him. He was calling the colt's name again and again and leaning forward, always watching the roan mare's head where she raced alongside.

The smoothness was gone out of Cedar's gait. Every tired muscle of him was in revolt, and he was racked with a mighty effort at every stride. Yet on and on he held and never slackened. Into the final hundred yards they came at last, with the lean gray head still on their flank. And now the sorrel labored hard, his sides all streaked with frozen sweat, his head and neck stretched out. But he paced on with weary legs.

Cut by the whip, the mare came up desperately, inch by inch. Bud knew that no whip could better the valiant fight the red pacer was making. "Cedar—Cedar, boy!" he cried, and to the anguish of his voice some last reserve of the colt's great heart responded, for his nose was still beyond Chocorua's when they lunged under the line of the wire.

·15·

DEATH DIVE

by STEPHEN HOLT

THE CHILL OF DAWN and a soft velvety horse nose on
his cheek awakened Leif. He sat up sharply, sending
two sparrows twittering madly off against the west wind.

"Big Red," he whispered, then reddened, pushing his
horse's head away. "I thought you were Big Red," he
said ruefully.

The brown horse snorted, then dropped his head to
pull at a tuft of dry grass.

Leif jumped to his feet and suddenly felt a bounding
confidence.

"This is the day I'll take him," he told Brownie, while
saddling and unhobbling him. "You won't mind spending a few days on the Run, will you? I'll be throwing my
saddle across Big Red and streaking out of here, pronto."

Brownie tossed his head and went on grazing, while
Leif quickly ate two slices of cold bacon between bread.

"There!" Leif quickly rolled his grub and blanket,
tying them on behind his saddle, then led Brownie down
to the creek and let the horse drink. While he, a few feet
upstream, did likewise.

In five minutes he swung a leg across the cantle of

his saddle and moved Brownie at a half-walk, half-trot off in the direction Waite so few hours before had taken.

Then began, as dawn changed to sunrise, to mid-morning, a duel between Leif and Waite with his riders.

Leif skirted a hill where he was sure Big Red might be. There were two Waite riders.

Big Red had been there. Now, he was a fleeing speck on the hills a mile south.

"We'll let the big guy run south," one of them jibed, twirling a handlebar moustache. "There's two riders there that'll head him."

The other rider's face broke into a swarthy grin.

Leif, without answering, swung his horse in a wide arc, and riding hard, succeeded in heading the band toward Magrath. For five miles he followed them, pressing his brown gelding to the limit.

Hope beat at him. For no Waite riders seemed in sight. Maybe he could haze the whole bunch into McCarty's corral—

Then suddenly, dipping into a swale, and coming up beyond it, he saw the band of horses stop sharply. Before Leif could more than swallow, they'd wheeled and came flying toward him. Two more of Waite's riders whooped after them.

Leif braced himself. He took down his lariat and raced toward them, whirling the rope over his head and shouting.

But he was only one against two seasoned punchers.

The band swept by him in wild disorder, Big Red leading, head outstretched, pistonlike legs sending his big red body over the prairie in a smooth flowing run that was beautiful to see.

Leif flung his rope in a wild desperate toss as Big Red passed. It sang out, and out, and out. And over—

For a moment, triumph filled Leif.

"I've got him," he yelled. Swinging his pony after Big Red, he soothed, "Whoa, boy! Whoa!"

But Big Red did not slacken his pace. With five mighty bounds he stretched the rope taut against the snubbed end of Leif's saddle. Another bound and he'd snapped it like a string and sped on.

Leif pulled Brownie to a walk, ruefully coiling the frayed end of his rope.

Waite's riders swept silently past him.

That suited Leif. He was angry clear through. All right, then! He turned and rode straight as an arrow toward Waterton Cliff. No use beating around the bush, he knew as he rode along. That was where Waite would take Big Red. That was where the show-down would be.

After a mile, one of Waite's riders turned back to Leif.

"Lad," he argued, dropping alongside Leif, "what chance have you against six hands that know their stuff?" His deep blue eyes under a worn Stetson glowed with concern. "Go on home and forget it."

Leif pushed on toward Waterton Cliff.

The rider pleaded, "Suppose you do snag Big Red. Even allow you saddle him before we get there. Waite'll just relieve you of him."

Leif did not answer. He put Brownie at a fast lope toward Waterton Cliff. It seemed sort of crazy with Big Red going off south again. But Leif played his hunch.

The rider made one last plea before following his partner after the fleeing horses.

"You figure to outsmart Waite," he said. "Don't try it."

Leif rode on, his thin blond face looking straight forward, his slender body following Brownie's steady canter.

"I can see you've got an idea—maybe ride Big Red off the Cliff," the rider persisted. "It's plumb crazy. No horse can take that jump and make it to Lost Island."

Leif turned his head.

"I know that," he said. "But I won't have to. Big Red'll make it up here—break through you guys circling him. When he does, I'll be there. I'll take him and ride right out from under your whole gang." He rode on.

The rider shaking his head and muttering, "Stubborn kid," swerved his horse and took up the chase for Big Red.

Leif rode on up to within a quarter of a mile of Waterton Cliff. Sitting under a big lone pine he stared out north to watch Waite's men, and Waite himself, try to corner Big Red.

Behind Leif lay Waterton Cliff. And below that the blue wind-riffled lake. Across the mile-wide lake was Lost Island. It wasn't really an island. It was a peninsula whose spruce-covered length hid the tiny thread of land connecting it with the United States land beyond.

From this United States side a trail led east along the side of Waterton Lake to the south end, then started upward, climbing toward Grizzly Pass—the only trail back to Canada and the town of Magrath.

Between watching Big Red racing his band of mares frantically from one side of the narrowing circle of Waite riders, and studying the changing cloud effects on Grizzly Pass and wondering what his chances on that Pass with Big Red might be, three hours passed by.

And then another hour, with the space left for Big Red to circulate growing less and less.

At last only the space of a quarter of a mile in diameter was left for the gallant horse.

Leif, watching from the back of Brownie, felt a sudden tightness at his midriff. In minutes now Waite would capture Big Red or else—

A fine sweat formed under Leif's hat. Scarcely knowing that he did, he wiped his forehead. And his blue eyes, deep with concern, never left Big Red's flying body.

Suddenly, a half-sob escaped Leif.

Big Red and his mares had only a scant hundred feet. The seven riders made a cordon of shouting rope-swinging riders who knew just how to handle the wild horses.

"No!" Leif whispered, watching Waite take down his rope. His hands automatically clenched his own, coiled at his saddletree.

Big Red ran straight at Waite, then swerved, his forefeet flashing in the dying sun, and ran frantically for the opposite side of the ring.

Waite followed, his rope loop swinging above his head.

Leif, from his distance, drew in his breath.

The rope sang out. Missed that big red weaving head.

Leif uttered a cry, and from sheer excitement raced Brownie along the hogback.

Suddenly, he checked Brownie and stared in unbelief. But in an instant burst into a loud shout of joy.

Big Red had plunged at the riders blocking his path. His great red body toppled two of them to the ground, then swept up the slope toward Leif.

On came the horse.

Waite and his riders abandoning the mares swept in pursuit.

Leif's heart drummed against his ribs.

Hey, the big guy would be winded at the speed he'd taken. He was pulling away from his pursuers. And— Leif's hand fell along his saddletree, the guy'd be easy to stop and saddle before Waite got there.

Leif figured out Big Red's path, then squeezed Brownie out of sight in a grove of quaking aspens, and waited.

On came Big Red.

Waite with his crew strung out behind him followed. A mile. A mile and a half.

Leif's stomach tightened under his belt, watching. It would be close, he knew. There would be a matter of seconds for him to stop Big Red and change the saddle. He reached down and loosened his cinch buckle. He loosed the throat latch on Brownie's bridle. Every move would count with Waite and his gang leaping toward them.

Now Leif could see the white of Big Red's eyes—his distended nostrils as he ran—his coat white with lather. A moment later, he swept past Leif. And Leif, a silent prayer on his stiff lips, sent Brownie in pursuit.

Big Red turned his head questioningly, then ran on.

Leif leaned forward in his saddle urging Brownie on.

For a hundred yards they ran without either gaining. The Cliff loomed ahead.

Leif shoved his heels to Brownie.

"Big Red," he called. "Big Red, whoa! Whoa, boy!" The big horse sped on.

Leif gave Brownie the rope end across his rump. The

brown horse leaped forward closing the gap between them.

He was gaining. Leif stood in his stirrups, then glanced backward. Waite rode less than two hundred yards behind. He was mad, yelling mad, and shaking his fists in the air as he came on.

Leif turned then, and gave Brownie the rope—

The Cliff seemed to leap at them, with Big Red leaping straight for it.

Then, Brownie overhauled the big red horse. Leif put out a hand for the frayed rope end he'd left on Big Red that morning. He clutched it. Took his dallies around his saddle horn, then set Brownie slowly to stop Big Red.

The big horse fought at first.

But Leif, running Brownie alongside, talked softly.

"Big Red—big boy. Whoa boy—"

And suddenly Big Red came to a halt.

The pound of hoofs rang from behind. Shouts filled the air.

Leif sprang to the ground and swept the saddle from Brownie and onto Big Red's foamy back.

Waite's voice came, "Quit it, kid. Cut it out!"

Leif swung the cinch under Big Red's heaving belly and catching it through the cinch buckle jerked it tight. The bridle came next with the pursuing hoofs pounding closer.

A sob escaped Leif. Would he just get Big Red bridled and saddled for Waite to grab? With trembling hands he slipped the bridle over Big Red's ears. Now, into the saddle. Leif grabbed the reins, his heart in his mouth.

The pounding hoofs—beating into his ears.

Leif shoved the boots to Big Red.

The big horse sprang free.

Waite surged alongside. He could just get his hands on the skirt of Leif's saddle, and clutch at the blanket.

Then the big horse's speed told. He ran straight away from Waite with Leif clinging to the saddle. But a hundred feet in the lead of Waite, Leif groaned as he swung the big horse to escape toward Magrath. For Waite's riders had fanned out and hemmed him in. Only the Cliff remained as a way of escape. The Cliff and Lost Island.

For an instant Leif hesitated. As the danger of the leap flashed through his mind, it was Waite's calling, "Run him down to the Cliff edge, boys—we'll take him there!" that decided him.

Leif swung the big horse straight at the Cliff, and standing up in the stirrups watched as it seemed to come sweeping toward him.

"Chris," he breathed, against the rush of the wind, and the startled cry of Waite: "You fool. You'll kill Big Red!"

There wasn't time for more.

He caught the edge of the Cliff in his eyes, tightened his hands on the reins and gathered his body along with Big Red for the leap. And the next instant the big horse came to the brink, hesitated for an instant, then shot forward.

Leif threw his weight with him. And together, horse and rider leaped out and down.

Leif felt the swift rush of air. Heard the frantic angry shouts of Waite above. And the next instant gasped with the cold rush of water over his head.

For hours, it seemed, they struggled through the water, then suddenly broke the surface.

214

Leif blew out, then caught his breath.

They went down again, bobbing like a huge red apple in a giant tub.

Three times they went under, then came up. Then suddenly, the big horse righted, caught his bearing and began a lusty swim toward the green fringe of trees that was Lost Island.

Leif looked back at Waite, sitting baffled and beaten on the Cliff. Boy, that had been close. For an instant, he felt relieved. Then swinging back to face the Island forgot his relief in what lay ahead. Cautiously then, he slid from Big Red's back off over his rump and catching hold of his tail, let the horse tow him toward Lost Island.

Climbing to the sandy shore and shaking the water from his clothes, Leif looked south and up at mist-drenched Grizzly Pass. A new sure light filled his eyes as he unsaddled Big Red and spread his blanket out to dry.

"Tomorrow, Big Red," he said to the horse, standing dripping and blown by the lake edge, "we'll go over that Pass. Then on to Lethbridge to win the Stockman's—"

°16°

JARVIS DISCOVERS GOLD

by GENEVIEVE TORREY EAMES

JARVIS SAT ON the wall eating the dry bread and the raisins and letting the warm sun sink into his shoulders. He was not thinking of anything in particular; it was enough to know this was the beginning of nearly three long months of vacation. There would be time enough for planning and doing things later.

On the far side of the pasture he could see half a dozen mares with their foals. Several of the foals were stretched out flat on their sides, sleeping soundly. Two others were having a game of tag, running in big circles around their mothers. Even at this distance Jarvis could see that the colts had grown amazingly since he had made his last visit to the pasture several weeks ago.

One black mare stood near the group, her head slightly on one side, her ears moving as the colts ran past her. That was old Lady-be-good, mother of some of the finest colts that High Acres had ever produced. She had been blind for three years, but she knew every stone and tree in the pasture and was able to get about with perfect safety. She depended a lot on her ears, and she seemed to enjoy listening to the colts as they dashed about. Her own foal was late this year; it was not expected for nearly a month.

Apart from the mares and dozing in the shade of a huge oak tree stood the two black Shetlands, Pepsi and Popsi. The girls had long since outgrown the ponies, but they refused stubbornly to give them up; so they would probably spend the rest of their lazy lives at High Acres. Jarvis sometimes rode Pepsi, but it was not much fun to go along with the girls on their faster horses and usually he didn't bother. He liked to watch the horses, though, and he liked to be with them and make friends with them. He liked grooming them and making their coats shine; he even liked cleaning the stables.

Beyond the ponies and partly hidden by the tree trunk Jarvis caught a glimpse of yellowish white that must be Joker, the three-year-old that was his particular pet. Joker was a misfit at High Acres. His mother had been bought for Mary to ride but had not proved satisfactory and was soon replaced by Gee-Whiz. Before she could be sold, however, she had surprised everybody by having a colt—a queer, awkward-looking thing, dingy cream in color. The mare had been sold in the fall, but nobody wanted the ugly little colt and he had been kept on through the winter and the two following years. Chet, the High Acres trainer, had been too busy with the more valuable colts, and Joker's education had been put off. Only Jarvis had bothered with him.

Jarvis finished the raisins and gave a piece of bread to Jack. He tried one of the carrots, but it was old and tough and he stopped after a couple of bites. He stood up and gave a long, shrill whistle. Several of the mares raised their heads and looked in his direction. After a minute they went on grazing. The two Shetlands paid no attention, but the light-colored colt under the oak moved a little way and stood listening. Jarvis whistled again and the colt stepped out from the shade of the tree.

As the sunlight struck Joker's coat, Jarvis took a deep breath. "Jeepers!" he exclaimed. "That can't be Joker!" He repeated the whistle and the colt started toward him.

"It is Joker, all right. But what's happened to him, I wonder? He never looked like that before."

The little horse stopped a short distance from the boy and stood like a statue, head outstretched, ears forward, nostrils sniffing to make sure this was a friend. The sun turned his coat to gold, except for the narrow white strip down his face and the two white socks on his hind legs. His mane and tail were silvery white and his eyes were dark and full, set far apart.

"Gosh!" Jarvis said, almost in a whisper. "You're— you're *beautiful*."

He held out the partly eaten carrot and the colt came slowly, a step at a time. "Wait," he said as the colt's muzzle reached toward his hand. "Have you forgotten everything I taught you? How old are you?"

Joker bent his head and pawed three times with his unshod forefoot.

Jarvis gave him the carrot and stroked his neck as he ate it. "I know," he said. "It's your coat; you've shed all your old winter coat since you were turned out to pasture, and your new summer coat is darker and yellower. Gee, it's like gold! I never thought you'd look like this,

219

and I bet nobody else thought so. You're my own dis-
covery."

Joker was sniffing at the boy's pockets. Jarvis touched
him on the foreleg and made him lie down. Then he sat
on the colt's shoulder and petted him.

"I've got to think up some new tricks to teach you,"
he said. "I bet there isn't anything you couldn't learn.
You could be a circus horse—you're smart enough. But
I'm afraid Mom and Dad would never let me join a
circus."

He let Joker get up, and gave him the rest of the
carrots. Then he sat on the ground and watched the colt
as he wandered slowly away, grazing as he went. He
imagined Joker, groomed and shining, his silvery mane
and tail washed and brushed, with a red bridle and sur-
cingle—and crowds applauding and cheering as he went
through his act. But his name wouldn't be Joker; that was
too plain. It would be—well, Gold Nugget or maybe
Gold Strike. Gold Nugget—that would look swell printed
on the programs. Everybody would be talking about
him. Jarvis knew it was only a dream, but he was fond
of dreaming; he didn't expect his dreams to come true.

Suddenly he realized it must be almost time for supper. With one last look at Joker he stood up and turned
toward home. He did not need to speak to Jack; the old
collie's head was at his knee before he had taken three
steps, and he reached down to give him a friendly pat.
He slipped into the house through the side door, and in
the little lavatory off the hall he stopped to look in the
mirror before deciding to wash his face. There was a
smudge of dirt across his nose, but the rest of his face
was reasonably clean; so he dashed a small quantity of

water where it would do the most good, and then dabbed at it carefully with one corner of the towel. There, he guessed that would get by.

It was a rainy morning, and Jarvis was curled up on the window seat in the living room hunting through old copies of *Rider and Driver* for a picture of a horse that looked like Joker. Not having found any, he put down the last number and began on a pile of *Western Horseman* magazines. Jack lay drowsing on the rug near by, his muzzle resting on his white forepaws.

The girls were in the room upstairs going over their plans for the horse show, and every now and then running to the telephone in the hall to call up the Stevenses and talk to Tad or Christine.

Mom was making out a shopping list for her next trip to town, and Dad was at his desk going over the farm accounts—a job he always saved for rainy days.

Mr. Dane looked up from his work. "Put down fence staples and some eight-penny nails, will you, Marty?" he said. "And see if Cushing has any colt halters; we need three or four."

Mrs. Dane nodded and went on with her list, while her husband sat staring at the books for a few minutes. "You know, Marty," he said, "we'll have to cut down on horses this year. Hay looks like a short crop, I'm afraid, and the price will be high. We ought not to keep any more stock than we can feed with our own stuff; it's poor business buying it from outside. I think we'd better let those two chestnut yearlings go. They aren't too promising. And we'll keep only a couple of weanlings—the best ones."

221

"I guess you're right," Mrs. Dane said with a sigh. "The worst thing about horses is you never want to part with any of them, even if you know you should."

"Then there's the cream three-year-old. If we don't get him broken, we'll have to sell him for dog meat."

"Oh no, Dad!" Jarvis exclaimed, sending a pile of magazines cascading to the floor as he jumped up.

"Keep your shirt on, son. You know I don't mean it. But that colt should have been broken before this. Nobody wants to buy a three-year-old that isn't even started —and not much of a horse at that. It's too bad he's such a poor color."

Jarvis opened his mouth to say something, but he closed it again.

"Marty," his father went on, "if Chet can find time to work on that colt for a week or so, couldn't you and the girls ride him around enough so we can sell him as green-broke? We'll lose money on him anyway, but at least we won't be feeding him next winter."

"Can't we keep him, Dad? *Please!* I—he's kind of a pet."

His father looked at him for a moment before he answered.

"We can't afford to keep horses just for pets. The girls ride theirs, and your mother and I ride ours. We're already keeping two ponies we don't need—you can make pets of them. If you wanted a horse to ride, it would be different."

"But Joker's so—well, he's like a *friend.*"

His father smiled. "I know. That's the way horses are. They're like people and you hate to let them go. But I'd have to be a millionaire to support all the horses we'd like to have, and we do need to be a little hardheaded sometimes—or give up raising horses."

"Don't worry, Jarvis," his mother put in. "Joker has a gentle, friendly disposition; he'll make a grand horse for children after he's broken, and we'll be careful to sell him to people who'll be good to him."

Jarvis looked back at the picture in his hand. In spite of himself his eyes filled with tears and he had to wink hard several times before he could see clearly. There it was, the horse he had been looking for. A beautiful Palomino, golden in color, with silver mane and tail—just like Joker, even to the white markings. He cut out the page and studied it for a minute before he slipped it into his scrapbook. This would be Joker in another year or two, when he was full-grown. And now—oh gosh!—he'd belong to somebody else, maybe somebody who wouldn't appreciate him.

He looked from his father to his mother and back again. It was no use; Dad was right, of course. A horse was expensive to keep, and it did sound silly to talk about having one around just for a pet—when there were always at least a dozen other horses on the place. Even a trick horse wasn't much good around a farm. Maybe there was some way Joker could be useful. If he were broken to harness he could earn his keep cultivating the garden.

But that idea was no good and Jarvis gave it up immediately. He could not imagine his proud, beautiful Joker dragging a cultivator up and down the corn rows.

Slowly he piled the magazines back on the bookshelves. He must think of something—some way to keep Joker at High Acres. He put his scrapbook under his

223

arm and went up to his room, Jack padding along behind him. Across the hall he could hear his sisters talking in a low hum. Maybe they would have an idea; anyway, he knew they would be sympathetic in a case like this. Anything that had to do with horses . . .

He crossed the hall and stood in the open doorway looking at the twins.

"Come in," Martha said, looking up briefly from a penciled list of exhibitors she was checking.

Mary had a big sheet of brown wrapping paper spread out on the floor. "I wanted to make a poster for the show," she said, "but I'm getting nowhere fast. Got any good ideas, Jar?"

"Could I do it myself? I'd like to. I'd do several, all different. Just tell me what printing you want on them."

"Gee, that would be swell! I never was any good at that sort of thing."

"They'll take a little time; I'll have to think about them first. How soon do you have to have them?"

"Oh, there's no hurry really. It's six weeks before the show, and I think we should get them up about two weeks beforehand. I was working on it now 'cause it's raining and there's not much else to do."

"How many classes are you going to have?"

"Wait. Martha's got the list. Here . . . 'Children's ponies under twelve hands. Ponies over twelve hands and under fourteen-two. Children's saddle horses. Ladies' saddle horses. Trail horses. Hunters. Children's hunters. Open jumping. Farm teams. Draft mares and foals. Lightweight mares and foals.'"

"We could have more classes," Martha said. "Maybe we will if enough people want to enter, but it's no fun having a lot of classes with only two or three horses in each one."

"And don't forget the prizes," Mary said.

"That's right. We've got to dig up a first prize for each class, besides all the ribbons."

"Where are you going to get the money for prizes?" Jarvis asked.

"We'll use the entry fees as far as they go," Martha answered. "We thought we'd get some good horse books —they make the best prizes for the least money. And a cup for the championship. If we don't have enough to cover it, we'll ask Dad to help out."

"Don't expect much from him," Jarvis said. "He's feeling awful poor—he's talking about selling off a lot of horses."

"What ones?" asked Mary.

"Not Annabelle!" Martha exclaimed.

"No, just colts," Jarvis answered. "And—and Joker."

"Gee, that's tough." Mary's face was troubled and she chewed the end of one braid, as she always did when she was upset. "You kinda counted on Joker, didn't you?"

Jarvis nodded.

"What do you care?" Martha asked. "You don't really want a horse, do you? You never ride, and there're lots of other horses on the place."

"But Joker was special. He's not like any other horse. I've always felt he was mine, even if he didn't really belong to me."

"Maybe they won't sell him, after all," Mary said hopefully. "He's not broken, and he's not much on looks— maybe nobody will buy him."

Jarvis shook his head. "They're gonna break him now,

225

right away—as soon as it stops raining, I guess. Chet's gonna start him; and Dad wants you and Mom to ride him around some, so he'll do for children. He doesn't want to waste much time on him."

"Well, he isn't sold yet."

"He will be. Can't you think of something, Mary?"

"We could teach him some bad tricks, so nobody could ride him."

Jarvis walked across the room and looked out of the window while he thought this over.

"That won't do," he said. "He's too good a horse to spoil. And, anyway, he'd be an outlaw and Dad would shoot him, most likely."

"I can't seem to think of anything else, but maybe I'll get an idea."

"He'll be here for the horse show anyway. Look, Mary, how about a class for trick horses?"

"Nothing doing," Martha broke in before Mary could answer. "He'd be the only one in the class and it would look as if we just wanted you to get a prize."

"I don't care about any prize—not even a ribbon. I just want him to show what he can do."

"Well, maybe, if there's time in the program. But it's a crazy idea. If he's so smart, it will just help to get him sold."

"He's going to be sold anyway, and I want him to be famous. Maybe somebody will buy him for the movies."

"Don't be silly. There aren't any movie people in this part of the country and, besides, a horse has to be more than smart to get in the movies. He's got to be glamorous."

"Horses aren't glamorous," Mary said. "At least they don't call it that."

"Well, you know what I mean. Who'd want Joker? He's got to be something extra for looks—like Roy Rogers' horse, Trigger."

"Trigger's a Palomino," said Jarvis slowly. "Gee, he's a grand horse—and smart, too."

"Well," Martha said, gathering up the scattered papers and putting them in order on the table, "Joker isn't Trigger."

"No-o-o," Jarvis agreed. "But—have you seen him lately?"

"Not since the horses were turned out to pasture. I guess it's over a month ago. Why?"

"Oh, nothing. You'll see him soon enough when Chet starts training him."

Jarvis picked up the sheet of wrapping paper and carried it back to his own room. He took the picture out of the scrapbook and propped it up on the desk in front of him. Then, leaning his arms on the desk, he stared at the picture. Jack sat down beside him and rested his chin on the boy's knee.

Jarvis patted the dog's head absently, his eyes still on the picture. "I've got to think of something," he said. "I've just got to."

Several days passed before Joker was mentioned again. Mr. Dane and the men were haying, and Jarvis hoped they would be so busy there would be no time to start training Joker. Every day he filled his pockets with carrots and oats and slipped off to the pasture with Jack, and nobody thought to ask him where he was going. The girls were so taken up with their plans for the show that they paid no attention to Jarvis. Even Mary seemed to have forgotten that she was going to try to think of some way to keep the colt from being sold. Jarvis himself was no nearer a solution.

But the lull ended at last. Sunday was a perfect June day and the family were eating a late breakfast on the porch. Mr. Dane set down his coffee cup and took a pack of cigarettes out of his pocket.

"Well, kids," he said as he struck a match, "what say we all stroll over to the hill pasture after breakfast? I haven't had a look at the colts in a long time and I'd like to see if they are coming along all right. Then we can get Joker and bring him down to the barn. Maybe Chet can get started on him this evening."

"Can we ride?" the twins cried together.

"Gosh, you two would get on a horse to cross the street! Sure, you can ride if you want to. Watch out, though; I've heard of people losing the use of their feet just because they never walked anywhere."

"I think it's a grand idea," Mrs. Dane said. "I'll be with you in half a sec. Come on, girls—let's get the table cleared first."

Jarvis looked at his father as the others left the table. "Do you suppose you could wait just a little while?" he asked. "There's something I want to do first. Could I go ahead, and the rest of you come in about half an hour?"

"Sure, anything you say. I'll help the girls with the dishes. They'll be so surprised they'll forget to ask where you are."

He went off to the kitchen, and Jarvis heard the twins shrieking with laughter when he asked for an apron.

Jarvis ran to the barn as fast as he could go. He still had no plan to keep Joker from being sold, but he felt it was up to him to see that the colt made a good impression.

"I've always been the only friend he had," he said to himself. "Nobody else ever appreciated him."

In the barn he gathered up a rubber currycomb, two brushes, a coarse mane comb, and a soft cotton cloth. He picked out one of his father's fancy show halters and a rope, and went off at a dogtrot through the woods to the pasture.

Joker, who was near the wall, snorted and ran as the boy came out of the woods. But when he recognized Jarvis he came back, his big dark eyes full of curiosity. Jarvis dropped the brushes on the ground and slipped the halter on Joker's head. Then, picking up the brushes, he looked around for a good place to tie the colt.

While Mary and Martha stopped to get their horses and lead them through the barway, their mother and father had gone ahead.

Nelson Dane's face was thoughtful as he strode along. "I wonder what that boy's up to," he said. "I know he's fond of that fool colt. You don't suppose he's hatched up some wild scheme to hide him so he can't be sold?"

"Oh, I don't think so, dear; but you never know what goes on in their minds. I'm puzzled about him—a boy so fond of horses never wanting to ride. Of course he's not particularly bold or venturesome; I mean he doesn't climb trees or take chances the way the girls do. But we have tried to encourage him about riding and it does no

229

good. The horses are just friends of his and he seems perfectly happy about it."

"Friends, yes. He seems to understand them even better than the girls do. He was the one who named Joker, remember? He claimed the colt knew he was funny-looking and that he made a joke of it."

"He may be right, at that. He was about the funniest little fellow we ever had on the place, and the most original. I'll never forget the time he grabbed Chet's cap and raced all around the paddock, shaking it and tossing his head and keeping his eye on Chet all the time to see what would happen. He was more like a mischievous puppy than a colt."

"He wasn't always so funny. How about the time he got the henhouse door open and went in and chased the hens off the nests and ate all the laying mash? We were three days getting the stray hens back, and some of them were so badly scared they never did lay again."

"All the same, Nelson, I wonder if maybe Jarvis isn't entitled to a horse of his own, just as much as the twins, even if he doesn't want to ride it?"

"I can't quite see it. We've always let them have all the pets they wanted, within reason. Everything from snakes to ponies—it goes with living on a farm. Jarvis has Jack, too, a one-man dog if ever there was one. You've got to draw the line somewhere."

"Yes, I suppose so. Listen—here come the girls."

The twins were riding single-file along the narrow trail, their voices rising happily above the sound of their horses' hoofbeats. As they drew near, their parents stepped out of the path to let them pass.

"They do have such good times together," said Mrs.

Dane, smiling. "It's too bad Jarvis doesn't have a twin. It seems to me he misses a lot of fun."

When they reached the edge of the woods, the girls were sitting on their horses near the barway and calling loudly for their brother.

Jarvis emerged after a moment from behind a clump of small pine trees.

"Wait a minute," he said. "Everybody stay there, please. I'm almost ready."

Mr. and Mrs. Dane sat down on the wall; the two girls relaxed, letting their horses crop the short grass near the bars.

Jarvis disappeared again, but soon came out leading Joker—a Joker groomed and polished until his golden coat gleamed in the sun. His silvery mane and tail were spotless, every hair in place. The colt carried himself proudly, his neck arched, his feet almost dancing on the soft turf. Jarvis posed him carefully in front of his parents and then looked anxiously at their faces. He had to smile at what he saw.

"Suffering cats!" his father exclaimed. "We never had a horse like that! Has our son taken to horse stealing, Marty?"

Mary almost fell off of Gee-Whiz in her excitement. "Oh!" she said softly. "Oh, gee whizz!"

Martha's mouth opened wide, and closed again before she could speak. "Why, he's—he's out of this world," she said. "He's a movie horse."

"He's beautiful," Mrs. Dane said. "He's like the Ugly Duckling in the story. I don't know what's happened to him, but, whatever it is, it's not possible!"

Jarvis grinned. "He's a Palomino," he said. "We just

didn't know it—that's all. I've been reading all about them; they've got a club, the Palomino Horse Association, with pedigrees 'n' everything."

"It's not only his color," his father said. "He's developed—filled out. I don't know when I've seen a colt change so. Last year I'd have traded him for a bale of hay, and now look at him!" He got off the wall and walked slowly around Joker, examining him carefully from all sides. "He's got darn good conformation," he went on. "I don't know where it came from; certainly his mother didn't amount to much. If he's properly schooled he'll make a show horse. I shouldn't wonder if we could get a pretty good price for him, after all. Well, son, you sure had a surprise for us."

"That isn't all," Jarvis said. "He's educated, too. Just watch."

He made Joker tell his age, bow, lie down, stand on his hind legs, pull a handkerchief out of Jarvis' pocket, and answer questions by shaking or nodding his head. Joker gave a perfect performance and seemed to be enjoying it as much as Jarvis.

The girls were delighted—and a little envious, too, because they had never thought of teaching tricks to their horses.

"Well, son," Mr. Dane said, "how about taking your pet down to the barn? Or do you want to walk over with us to look at the foals?"

Jarvis shook his head. "I've seen them 'most every day. And, besides, if Joker's got to go to the barn, I'd better take him now, by himself."

"All right. Just turn him into the paddock until Chet's

ready for him. Come on, girls—tie your horses there in the shade and let's go over to see the babies."

Jarvis let down two bars and led Joker out. The twins tied their horses, then helped Jarvis replace the bars.

"He's swell," Mary said, stopping to pat Joker before she joined her father. "I don't blame you for wanting him. But honest, Jar, I can't think of any way to manage it. Maybe we'd better have a private meeting and talk it over."

"In the loft?"

"Sure—after dinner. I'll tell Martha."

The excitement over, Jarvis was feeling pretty glum as he led Joker through the woods toward the barn. It was all very well for Mary to call a meeting in the loft, where only the most important and secret conferences were held—nevertheless, she hadn't sounded very hopeful. As long as Joker's training was merely talked about, there had been a chance—just the slightest chance—that it might be postponed again and again. And, as long as the colt remained in the pasture, nobody had known what he looked like. But now the secret was out. Now that Dad and Mom knew what a handsome horse they had, there was no hope at all.

Jarvis wondered how long the training would take. A horse as smart as Joker might be considered "green-broke" in a couple of months. He opened the paddock gate and closed it carefully behind Joker.

"What you got there?" a voice called from the barn.

Chet put down the pail he was carrying and came out toward the paddock. He was a small, wiry man with grizzled hair, and his light blue eyes had crinkly lines at the corners. He was wearing faded tan breeches and riding boots and an old gray cap. He moved slowly and talked quietly, but he could be quick when quickness was needed.

"It's Joker. Dad said you were going to train him."

"Hmph! He's turned out right purty, ain't he? Beautiful but dumb, most likely."

"He is not! He's the smartest colt we ever raised!"

"Ornery, then. No horse could be that good-looking and not have something wrong with him." Chet's face looked serious, but Jarvis decided he was only fooling.

"What do you think of him, Chet? Really, I mean."

"Tell you better after I've worked on him for a week or so. He *looks* good; yep, he sure looks good. Say—you better put that show halter right back in the tack room."

"I only borrowed it while I showed him to Dad; *he* didn't care."

Jarvis slipped the halter off Joker's head and turned him loose.

The colt stood for a moment with upraised head, looking off toward the pasture. He neighed once, and listened. There was an answering neigh from one of the horses in the stable, but he paid no attention. He walked around the paddock sniffing at the ground. Then he flung up his head and broke into a fast, springy trot, his tail held high and streaming out like a flag. He circled the paddock twice and finally, as if he had made up his mind, he galloped straight for the four-foot fence, cleared the top rail with inches to spare, crossed the drive, and jumped the bars on the other side. Before Jarvis could speak, he had disappeared into the woods.

Jarvis turned to look at Chet. The trainer's face wore an expression of surprise that was almost funny. There was a look of real interest, too, and Jarvis felt suddenly proud and happy. When Chet looked *that way* at a horse —well, it meant a lot.

Chet took off his battered cap and scratched his head.

"I'll be durned," he said. "As clean a jump as I ever saw! Jumped right off his hocks, too, like he's been doing it all his life. Don't know but I could make something of that colt."

Jarvis drew a deep breath. If Chet liked him—if Chet really worked on him—Joker would be the best-trained horse in the county. "I—I guess I'd better go get him," the boy said.

•17•

CORRAL WALLS

by DAVID GREW

ROLLING HILLS and shadow valleys—an ocean of brown waves with fast-drying sloughs, like patches of sunshine on the bosom of the sea—such was the Canadian prairie that autumn day, such were the miles and miles of Alberta range, bounded by a barbed-wire fence which was completely lost in the unobstructed play of sunshine. It was an open wilderness which reached beyond the horizon. The horizon itself lay desolate and unbroken like a rusty iron ring, girdling the earth. The immensity of space, by contrast, dwarfed everything which crept over the surface of the plains into a helpless sort of puniness.

The hundred horses on the range, grouped and scattered by their likes and dislikes of each other, looked from the distance like ants crawling over the surface of a rock. Within sight of each other, bound as they were by the ties of race, they nevertheless had their loves and social preferences.

Most of the mothers with their little colts grazed to one side of the herd, out of the possible danger of being hurt by some outbursts of exuberance on the part of the young adult horses; and a few of the mothers among

237

these, as if they regarded their children as more precious than their neighbor's children, kept to themselves.

Among this last group was a shapely, light-brown or buckskin mare who was grazing peacefully around her delicate little buckskin daughter. The little thing was asleep on the grass. Her thin, graceful legs were stretched as far as she could stretch them. Her beautiful little head lay flat on the ground. Her fluffy tail was thrown back on the grass with complete abandon.

She was only six months old but already the very image of her mother. From the white strip on her forehead and the heavy black mane to the unequal white spots on her two hind fetlocks, she was like her. Only her wiry, delicately wrought legs seemed somewhat too long for her.

Suddenly the old mare's head went up high in the air. Her teeth ceased grinding with the abruptness of a machine which, in breaking, comes to an unexpected stop. Her round, knowing eyes peered anxiously through the warm haze in the atmosphere.

The small head on the grass also raised a little bit, looked inquiringly at its beloved mother, saw her quite near, and with absolute confidence in that nearness, dropped back again, rubbing its muzzle against the fragrant grass in an ecstasy of contentment.

But the old mare continued gazing suspiciously, remaining motionless—like a stone. She saw that most of the rest of the horses were as alert as she was, watching the small, moving objects—two men on horseback—which had broken over the line of shadow along the southern horizon.

One of the two men had loped off toward the right

The old mare continued gazing suspiciously

and the other toward the left. The old mare had already lived twenty years in the precarious relationship of horse to man. Not only had she herself suffered at the hands of these little creatures who ruled the world, but she had had many of her babies taken away from her and abused by them—several times before her very eyes. Her mother's heart began to beat fast and apprehensively.

The other mares, not far from her, began to show signs of extreme nervousness. Some began running off short distances, as if in panic, stopping every few feet and gazing anxiously at the approaching riders, putting their colts and themselves on guard with this show of fear.

The buckskin mare looked for a moment questioningly toward the north. That was the way to go, for the ranch buildings were in the south. But already the two riders, now to the side of them, were racing northward and she knew that they would get beyond them and turn upon them to drive them toward the ranch.

She called nervously to her little one with that strange tremulous whinny which she used only in time of danger. The filly sprang at once to her feet, sidled up to her mother, and from the protection of those big, warm, throbbing sides, peered wide-eyed at the tiny dark forms of the riders who were now coming together in the north.

Until she had seen a group of horsemen dismount one day, the little buckskin filly had thought that man was a strange sort of horse with a frightening hump on its back. What little she had been able to learn about him since had served only to intensify her fear of him; and despite her abiding confidence in her mother, she began to tremble as she heard the telltale hoofbeats coming nearer and nearer.

The horses all instinctively gathered together in a bunch and, since the riders were north of them, raced full speed toward the canyon in the south. But while one of the horsemen remained some distance behind them, ready to prevent the group from swerving to the side, the other one plunged right into their midst and cleverly separated the mothers and their colts from the rest of the herd. Then they allowed the single horses to run off northward as they pleased, and got together behind the mothers and their colts, driving them toward the canyon which, from the level plains where they were, looked like a snaky shadow just short of the horizon and parallel to it.

That long line of shadow widened as they neared it; and when they reached the lip of the canyon, they saw the shining, narrow stream of the Red Deer River, way down on its flat bottom. From the jaws of the mouth of the canyon which were more than a mile apart, the prairie floor fell away sheer in places to a depth of a thousand feet. Here and there, there were cuts in the canyon lip, ravinelike gouges in the level edge. Where the elements, throughout the ages, had failed to remove the loose earth, it lay along the slope in steep hills which rose from those slopes like giant teeth, crumbling more or less, dotted with stones and covered here and there with blotches of sagebrush and cacti.

In the middle of the flat canyon bottom, between the jagged slopes and the river shore, stood the mushroom-like buildings of the ranch. The house, a small wooden building with shingled sides, stood on the eastern end of the long ranch yard, while opposite and facing it, was the huge red barn with its open door below and the square, gaping window space in the loft above. North of the barn and against its blind wall, there was a big corral, divided into two sections by a partition. The corral walls as well as the partition were made of logs, laid horizontally about a foot apart and rising to a height of some six feet. Each of the two sections had heavy swinging gates which opened inward.

Helplessly, the mothers and their colts poured down the steep incline between the giant teeth, into the canyon, slipping, sliding and leaping riskily over the stones in their way.

On the level bottom of the canyon, the buckskin mare made an attempt to get beyond the rancher's buildings to the river, but one of the horsemen immediately shot by her like a flash of light, heading her off. She knew enough of the bitter futility of trying to balk against the will of man; and so she turned back into the dust-clouded stream of mothers and colts with an angry shake of her wise old head.

But whatever the old mare, wise in experience, felt about this excitement, since all they had had to do so far was run, the little buckskin filly shook all fear from her heart and clinging desperately to the protecting side of her mother, took what pleasure she could from the exhilaration of the escapade itself. Healthy to the last cell of her body, the race had merely accelerated the circulation of her blood; and the ease with which she found herself able to keep up with her mother made her conscious of a great and thrilling power within herself. Her eyes dilated, her nostrils distended, her mane bristling

243

and her tail unfurled, her springy legs carried her along, an expression of joy and abandonment in the motion of her graceful body.

The gates of the corral stood wide open. Being so driven that they could not swerve to either side, half the mothers and their colts poured into one section of the corral and half into the other. At the opposite walls of the corral, inside, finding no way of getting out, they stopped and turned to look back toward the gates, and they saw the two men closing them.

The knowledge that they were imprisoned, trapped in those unbreakable walls of heavy logs, terrified them. In their utter helplessness, they raced aimlessly around and around the corral, churning up the earth under their hoofs and filling the air with clouds of dust so thick that it became hard to breathe.

When the wiser ones realized that it was getting them nowhere and only adding to their discomfort, they settled back near the gates in a bunch and, looking over the corral walls and between the logs, watched the ominous activities of the two men in the yard.

They saw one man building a fire in the center of the yard; while the other was calmly manipulating a long iron rod, as if he were pawing the smoking flames with it.

The little buckskin filly, close against her mother's side, was wedged into the corner between her mother and the logs of the corral wall; her frightened eyes, in the middle of the space between two of the logs, could see the rancher's house on the other side of the yard.

Her flanks were still throbbing from exertion when the house door opened and she saw a little girl come out of it. The buckskin filly didn't know what kind of animal that was, except that she guessed it was a sort of man. She noticed with no little fear that the small girl was coming, hopping and skipping, directly toward the corral. The little filly pressed hard against her mother's side, but her mother, absorbed in the activities of the men, did not move an inch.

When suddenly the little buckskin felt the touch of the girl's hand on her back, she called out frantically to her mother. The old mare lowered her soft warm lips, carressed her on the forehead and along her back and neck, murmured reassuringly, but again raised her head over the top log and continued staring at the men.

By that time the filly realized that, uncomfortable as it was to have this little man-thing touching her, it was not hurting her. She decided to tolerate it, while her one dilated eye guarded against anything the little girl might do which *would* hurt.

Then the strange girl in her brightly colored dress climbed up two of the logs and moved slowly toward the frightened buckskin's head, talking softly and coaxingly as she moved.

The filly listened with ears pricked high. In the stream of meaningless prattle, the little filly became aware of one sound: the sound of the word "Queen," which the girl repeated many times. Somehow, as the girl repeated that word, more and more endearingly, the filly began to feel that there was no ill-will, no hurt of any kind in the intentions of the strange creature, and her fear turned to curiosity.

There was something very disarming about the soft voice which came through between the logs; and she cautiously put her muzzle through the space between the logs, toward the pink little face from which the soft sounds were coming. When the tremulous lip touched the warm skin, the girl turned abruptly and kissed it, crowing with delight. The filly pulled back, eyes dilating and ears pricked forward, but immediately reached toward her again; and the little girl, more excited than ever now, kept calling: "You're my little Queen; you're my little Queen."

This unofficial christening was interrupted by a sudden outburst of excitement on the other side of the partition. As the mothers and their colts in the other section broke into another helpless whirling around that side of the corral, the mothers and colts on Queen's side joined them in a similar, blind churning; and the clouds of dust shut out the yard and swallowed up the little girl.

For a quarter of an hour they raced around blindly, before they realized that the men were not interested in them nor their part of the corral. When they had withdrawn to the farthest corner of their section and the dust had settled somewhat, Queen saw a man on the other side of the partition rush toward a big black mare with a long stick. She saw him strike the colt that tried to follow the mare and saw the colt run back into the corral, while the mother was being driven out and away by the second man. In this way, the two men drove out all the mares and kept all the colts in the corral. The air was filled with the whinnies for help on the part of the colts, and the helpless answers from their mothers outside.

The mares and colts around Queen, frightened as they were, had moved off as far as they could in their own section of the corral and were looking on. Queen saw a rope flash through the air, and immediately after she saw a colt fall to the dusty ground with a cry to his mother for help. The anxious neigh which his mother sent through the air in response stirred the mothers in Queen's section of the corral, and they began whirling around the dusty square again, blindly expressing their desire to escape, yet so despairing of finding an opening in the sturdy log walls that they didn't even look for it.

When once more they slowed down and stopped in the farthest corner, there was a frightening odor of blood and burning flesh in the air. The smell of the branding further terrified them and again mothers and colts took to whirling foolishly around. As soon as they stopped again, another colt was thrown and branded, and again the cries of pain and fear and the smell of burning hide sent them racing through the dust.

It took the two men the greater part of the afternoon to brand all the colts in the first section of the corral; and when that half of their labor was finished, their faces wet with perspiration and black with layers of dust, the men retired to the ranch house for a few minutes' rest and a refreshing drink. By that time all the colts who had been branded had been released and with their frantic mothers were racing away up the incline to the freedom of the prairies on the range above.

The mothers and colts in Queen's section of the corral stood looking after them enviously till the last of them had vanished beyond the rim of the canyon.

A kindly silence lowered upon the ranch yard, and Queen, like most of the other colts in the corral, took advantage of the peace and quiet to help herself to her mother's milk. Before they were half through their supper, however, they were interrupted by the sudden re-appearance of the two men. The skin on the buckskin mare's flanks began to vibrate, and the old mare suddenly pulled away to plunge once more into the foolish and frenzied revolving around the dusty corral.

One man came through the big gate carrying a long stick, while the other man remained at the swinging gate holding it open slightly. The man with the long stick forced the mothers and their colts into one corner of the corral; then, after a long struggle, he singled out the buckskin mare, separating her from the rest and driving her toward the gate.

The old mare had gotten halfway out of the gateway when she heard the frantic cry for help from little Queen. Rebelliously rearing up on her hind legs, the old mare turned back. She struck the gate with all her weight, just as the man was trying to shut it behind her. The gate swung violently out of her way, knocking the gateman off his feet and striking with a crash against the corral wall.

The man with the big stick ran to help his companion up from the ground. The gateway open, Queen joined her mother. Out they all went as fast as they could go, the buckskin mare in the lead.

Before the man with the big stick had dragged his companion out of the corral, the mares and their colts were halfway up the incline of the canyon slope on their frenzied race for the range above, the buckskin mare now puffing and snorting as she beat her way up the steep grade, little Queen bravely pattering along after her. The old mare was very nervous. She was not only eager to get to the range with her little daughter, but she vaguely realized that she had crossed the man's will; and that, her experience warned her, was a punishable offense.

The men, on the other hand, had several disadvantages. Besides one of them having been weakened, almost incapacitated by the blow of the swinging gate, they knew that before they could resaddle their ponies, these mares and their colts would reach the flat prairie on the range above and join the other mares and their colts, and perhaps also the rest of the horses of the range. They realized, too, that after all the excitement of the day, the horses would be nervous and wary, much harder to round-up than ordinarily. The day was already waning; so they postponed the completion of the branding to some other day, when the mares and their colts had gotten over their fright somewhat.

Having no way of knowing that the two men were not going to pursue and recapture them at once, the rebellious mares and their colts raced recklessly up the incline, the perspiration coming out in foam upon their necks and sides, rocks and sand rolling thunderously down behind them, dust rising from their feet like the smoke of a prairie fire.

When they finally reached the level plains above the canyon, the old buckskin mare led the mothers and their colts westward. Having been rounded up in the hollow, directly north of them, she was wise enough to feel that the men would be sure to come back there to look for them. The desire to get under cover and keep out of sight sent her galloping anxiously for a deep ravine, a mile and a half to the west, where she remembered clumps of wild cherry trees deep down its steep slopes.

249

Although Queen now protested from time to time against the strain of so much loping, the old mare did not slacken her pace till she reached the deep cut in the prairie floor and saw the cherry trees in the V-shaped cut before her. And even here, though she slowed down considerably, she was not yet ready to rest. Trotting down to the old cattle trail, along the very bottom of the ravine, she continued going northward on it until the barbed-wire fence of the range forced her to end her flight.

Here at last they gathered into a bunch and, looking back guardedly, began to graze. The old buckskin mare, like most of the other mothers, kept a careful watch, continuously raising her wise old head and studying the rim of the ravine for the first sight or sound of approaching riders.

Most of the colts went back to their supper, so rudely interrupted in the corral; and when that evening meal was completed, each of them found a soft spot on the grass near where their mothers were grazing and, stretching out, went to sleep.

In a few hours, none the worse physically for the exertions of the day, Queen got up and proceeded to find grass for herself, as her mother had been encouraging her to do for some time. She was feeling extremely good after her rest, even better than she had ever felt before.

If Queen, however, was inclined to regard the wild chase over the prairie and down the canyon slopes to the ranch yard as an escapade, as so much fun, her mother's nervous watchfulness, which had not abated in the least, had nonetheless deepened the impression made upon Queen that man was a creature to be afraid of, to guard against. No matter how peacefully she appeared to be

grazing, the buckskin mare would stop every other minute, look back along the ravine to the top, or walk up to
the fence and with her head above the topmost strand
of barbed-wire, press her chest against the barbs and
look hungrily up the rest of the ravine and to the line of
the flat prairie above, stretching away indefinitely toward the north.

Where the V-shaped ravine bottom brought the two
slopes to a point, the barbed-wire fence was most allur-
ingly high. That spot fascinated the old mare. It gave her
the feeling that, with a little effort, she could push her
way under there and out of the range fence. Somewhere
in the back of her mind was a vague cluster of memories
of just such a situation, of a strand of wire hanging high,
of her getting down on her knees somehow and pushing
her way out to freedom.

She stood there for seemingly endless hours and gazed;
and when she wearied of doing that and after she had
gone off to the grazing which was a grim necessity, she
kept coming back to the wire, sniffing above and below
it and looking hungrily away into the north.

Sometimes, her fear of the riders becoming especially
intense, the buckskin mare would begin to imagine them
up there on the prairies above and behind her, and she
would suddenly go tripping up the west slope of the
ravine to get a long view of those plains. The rest of the
mothers, catching the contagious fear from her, would
go racing after her, their frightened colts at their sides.
Then, seeing no sign of any riders, she would lead them
back down to the ravine and take up her study of the
barbed-wire strands which were preventing her escape

to the north, away from the river canyon and the ranch yard.

Every time she returned to that fence, her memory of an experience with such a barbed wire in the dim past became clearer, and the impulse to try to get out became stronger. Finally, getting down on her knees, the old buckskin mare pushed her head under the lowest strand of wire and began slowly to reach forward. The sense of being on the other side encouraged her and she began crawling forward more and more eagerly, more and more nervously.

Then her withers struck a barb in the wire and the pain as it broke through the skin halted her a moment. Her intention now was to lower herself a bit more, out of its reach, when out of the rosebush just a few feet from her nose leaped a jack rabbit. In her fright, the buckskin mare sprang to her feet. The sharp burning pain in her withers as the barb ripped a cut several inches long gave her the feeling that she was caught in a trap. Foolishly she reared on her hind legs to pull out of it. The strand of wire snapped with a loud *ping* as from a tuning fork, one end of the broken wire tearing a gash along her shoulder.

Somehow, though her fright urged her back into the range and away from that wire, she found herself outside of the fence with the next upper strand of wire now behind her. Instead of going backward she sprang away northward, up the ravine.

Queen was afraid of the fence and the hanging wires, having been hurt by barbed-wire fences several times in the past; but the idea of being separated from her mother was unendurable. With a nervous, frightened

lope she ran under the wire and to her mother's side.
Soon one of the other mares came trotting along, afraid
and yet eager and bursting with curiosity. In a few
minutes the entire group was excitedly trotting up the
ravine slopes to the open prairies.

Up on the plains, free to lope northward away from
the direction of the ranch, they fled for the greater part
of an hour. But the colts were tired of this constant running and the old mares were hungry. The grass up on
those unoccupied wild prairies was especially high and
inviting; and so, coming to what seemed like a secluded
hollow, they stopped to graze.

While the buckskin mare went at her grazing as
greedily as the rest of them, she was far more nervous
than any of them. She had broken out of the corral and
she had broken out of the fence. Besides a guilty sense of
having resisted the will of man, her neck and shoulders
were hurting where the wires had cut her and the feeling
of warm trickling blood was frightening.

The late autumn nights had steadily grown colder, and
since the hollows are generally cooler than the higher
portions of the prairie ground, the coldness kept them
stirring around; and so the buckskin mare soon started
them on northward again. Grazing close together, lips
often touching lips as they seized the bunches of grass
and ripped them from the earth, they pushed slowly
northward. When the colts, too weary to go on any
farther, began lying down, one by one, they were some
four miles north of the range.

When dawn came the earth and the grass blades were
white with frost; the rising sun put a tinge of pinkish
lavender into the wide whiteness of the slopes which

253

faced it. The lazy colts who were still sleeping were soon awakened by the cold.

As more and more of the colts began getting up, those who were not particularly hungry, or were colder than they were hungry, began chasing each other in play, circling about the group of mares who were busily cropping the grass and moving along.

The old buckskin mare was glad to see them so active. The nervousness which had seized her when first the men had come to round up the mares and their colts was now greatly intensified by the large lumps of coagulated blood on her neck and shoulders, only a small portion of which she could reach with her lips. The loss of blood, much of which had trickled down her foreleg, put her into an extreme state of apprehension which gave her no peace unless she was in flight. Time after time she led the herd on a frightened race northward until the unwilling older mares and some of the tired colts would rebel. Then she was obliged to stop again and graze a while.

Moving along in that way, all morning, they came toward noon to a slough where the grass around a large oval pond was so high and luscious that there was little chance of dragging the herd away from it. Trying to lead them on again, after they had drunk their fill, the buckskin mare finally settled down on the north slope of the hollow and grazed like the rest, interrupting her grazing constantly with anxious looks southward, trying each time she looked up to get at the painful wounds on neck and shoulder.

It was in the middle of the afternoon that the old mare was disturbed by the sound of honking geese. Looking up, she found them in the north sky, their familiar V-formation moving across overhead and southward. The buckskin watched them anxiously as long as their constantly growing-smaller specks were visible.

She was about to go back to her grazing when right below the last tiny speck, a short distance above the southern horizon, she discovered two small dark objects coming toward them over the prairie. The men were coming again! She watched them just long enough to have other mares become concerned and look up like her; then with her nervous frenzied call, which the herd had come to know so well, she loped around in a wild circle till she had the whole group sufficiently worried; then she galloped away to the north, Queen at her side, the herd directly behind her.

Until the herd showed signs of wearying of the chase and she herself, weakened by the loss of blood, could feel the blood trickling again from the wound on her neck, the buckskin mare galloped and trotted by turns. On a wide ridgetop they grazed for about half an hour. Suddenly, looking up, the buckskin mare saw the men on horseback coming again, this time considerably nearer.

She had little difficulty arousing the herd this time. Old mares and lazy colts, all thoroughly alert, eyes dilated and nostrils distended, they began their flight northward in real earnest.

For several hours they fled into the heart of a vast, unpopulated wilderness. When the shadows of the early autumn evening began lengthening to the side of them, they came to a hilltop from which they saw another one of those prairie sloughs with a good-sized pond shimmering in its muddy center. Here they stopped to drink and to graze, remaining till long after the night had settled down; then they moved on again.

They came late in the night to an old abandoned haystack in the middle of a swampy hollow. As the buckskin mare, now terribly weak and tired, stopped to survey the field and the shadowed stack, the night lay over the land like a flood of solid darkness. Not a single light gleamed anywhere in the black distances of the prairie, nor was there a trace in the air of any barnyard smell. She could make out a number of horses resting against the hay, and she could see one or two grazing a short distance to the side.

A cold wind had blown up from the west and the buckskin mare wanted to get into the protection of the haystack. She moved forward a few feet and stopped to sniff; and the herd moved along cautiously behind her. Several times they moved forward in that manner, stopping each time to make sure, and then the buckskin mare saw the shapes of several horses lying at the base of the stack.

The haystack was a very old one, abandoned several years ago, and the smell that came from it was half rotten; but with the pungent odor of rotten hay came the smell of warm horse bodies, and the buckskin called out inquiringly.

In answer to her call a white body close to the stack raised itself laboriously from the ground and, taking a step forward, replied with a lazy, sleepy whinny. Immediately the buckskin mare and the little group back of her, started forward toward the haystack.

The buckskin mare found the white body to be a good-natured white mare and as soon as they had sniffed noses, the white mare hurried back to her warm place before it was taken from her. Beside her, as Queen's mother followed her to the stack, was a jet black colt who was complaining impatiently because his mother had disturbed his sleep by getting up.

The hay was too old to be appetizing, but they had not come there to eat. What they wanted was shelter from the penetrating wind which was especially tormenting the buckskin mare by probing at her open wounds. As soon as the first formalities of whinnying assurances were over, each mare and her colt went looking for the warmest place still available along the haystack.

In her eager search in the darkness, the buckskin mare almost stepped on the leg of an old work horse, but the old fellow whinnied good-naturedly and she decided to lie down right beside him. Queen pushed herself into the hay between the old work horse and her mother; thus protected against the wind, she was soon very comfortably cosy and fell asleep.